The
Forest
Whisperings

The Lost Legacy

The Forest Whisperings

NESH

PARTRIDGE

A Penguin Random House Company

To order additional copies of this book, contact
Partridge India
000 800 10062 62
orders.india@partridgepublishing.com

www.partridgepublishing.com/india

Contents

Avantika

Sanjay

Acknowledgement...

I am really grateful to my parents and my brother for allowing me to go ahead with my dreams in writing my novel. It has been the best of days and nights, when I inked these words first at our place.

If I had come till writing this acknowledgement, it's only because of you three: Nandita NH, Vertika Saxena and Bharath Keerthi. From the first word till the end of the book, it has been an enjoyable journey, thanks to you three. Nandita, you had made sure that I did not loose my focus, even in the hardest times. There have been several calls, which ended just to make sure I didn't deviate from my track. Vertika, it was your motivation and constant corrections that made me finish this book. It's you who gave me the first review to my book, which will stay in my heart forever. Whether it was our late night discussions or the debate over the characters, Bharath I couldn't have done it without you. You were my editors before my publishers.

It would not have been this great if Ram Arvinth, Shreyas, Suriya Prabha, Suganya, Aydhika, LGS (Lakshmi) and Atmajah hadn't suggested me tips in developing the characters. If you are stuck to these characters till the end, it's all from them.

I thank Harini Kailash and Thanveera for being brave enough to point out my mistakes and helping me in rectifying them.

Cheers to my friends Rajagopal, Sreenesh, Krishna and Ashwin for taking my burden on their shoulders during my seventh semester. Mind you, it is not easy to work in Flight testing lab.

Venkateswaran, Nishanth(Saamiyar), Krishna(Tom), Bala, Sajin, Sankar(mama), Rajasekar, Tahir and Revathy: You have been my first motivation from school. I love you guys. If there was a part of my life I want to relive, it will be my schooldays with all you people.

My interest in music grew after listening to your music. Ramakrishna, Vignesh Shekar, Sharmila and Aditya; you people should start a band.

My acknowledgment won't be complete if I don't mention these names: Suresh Sharma, Aditya and Ashwin Reddy for being there when I needed.

Special thanks to SBOA Matriculation and Higher Secondary school and Amrita School of Engineering for raising me with such wonderful sets of friends.

My special thanks to Penguin Patridge publishers for making my dream come true. The way you people approach a fresh author just motivates him to reach higher heights.

My sincere thanks to Joe Anderson, Bryan Carter and Nancy Avecedo for being the guiding lights in my path of becoming a writer.

Last but not the least, a salute to you readers for choosing this book and hope you stay with my characters.

Dedicated to
Krishnamurthy
Sudha
Prasanth
Nandita
Vertika
Bharath
And JKR for making me explore the magic of books

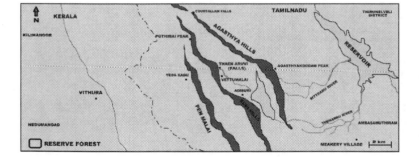

0
7292 BCE

Southern India

He was looking at the sea. The shores that had made his clan's life prosper. The wealth he got from the sand and seas. But that is not what he is worried about. It is about the information he received from his sacred father.

'Oh son, under your rule, the land will grow in immense wealth and power. But we have gone to the heights where even Gods are afraid to tread! When Varuna, the Lord of the seas is furious, he won't leave the land you rule. Move with your people and leave in search of new land where you can build your kingdom from dust.'

He looked around. His people gathered in front of the palace to listen to their beloved king. He has to break down the news, the news his people feared the most. Many have become sick because of the unknown forces that radiated from the *kanimam*, the wealth he obtained from the sea shore. Many have lost their skin texture, their eye sight, grown old quickly and even died because of the effect from the unknown force. Despite the wealth on trade of this mineral made into weapons to the Rishis and Kings of Northerly states of Ayodhya, Anga and Gandara, he has ordered his workers to extract all the *kanimam* and pile it away from the people, inside the deep forest. At least the future kings won't do the mistake he did and the people can be safe from these unknown forces. But the Lord of the Seas is not happy.

His priests have been doing several Yagas to please the lord of seas.

'Aum Jalbimbaye Vvidmahe

Nila Purushaye Dhimahi

Tanno Varunah Prachodayat'

The mantra was being constantly chanted by his priests. But the rains didn't stop at all.

Recently the visit from the Sage Vishwamitra, who had taught the art of using this weapon to Lord Rama himself, conveyed him that Lady Sita has been abducted by the Evil King of Lanka, Ravana. Furious Rama had left the Dandaka forest with his brother Lakshmana and his army towards Lanka.

He looked down at the people again. Despite the heavy rain, they have gathered down the palace. They knew it. Their faces told that. But they hoped that their king had a solution. He began speaking.

'My dear people, the time has come. Our worst fear has come to us in the form of water. This land, our land, will be consumed by Lord Varuna. We have destroyed our once beautiful land. The crops are no longer sprouting in our land. Our once proud and tall coconut trees are now producing poisonous waters. People are dying every other day because of the evil force coming from the kanimam. Our doctors are unable to find a cure for this disease.' he paused, 'When the moon has grown to its fullest size, with the things we have in our hand, let us move towards inner land of Bharath in search of our new home.' He finished.

The King mounted his mighty elephant with huge tusks. It had been his friend ever since he got it at the age of 12. He had come to the Varuna temple to offer his final prayers. The royal guards were vested in leather with a sword in one hand and the empire shield in the other. The shield had the emblem of a mighty tusker engraved on it. He had been a fair ruler, whom the people always loved. He removed his crown for having failed to save his land and placed it on the Garbagriha of the temple at Lord Varuna's feet.

Sea had become rough in the past few days. Today the water receded further away from the shore. All the boats that were in the sea hit the ground. Few people didn't want to leave the land that raised them. The King and most of the people had left their land and went in search of their new home. People who stayed back were in their Varuna temple.

The sages from the temple were saying that Lord Varuna had given a way for Rama to cross the sea.

Waves taller than their coconut trees were rushing towards the city. It was flushing down their city wall consuming anything that came its way. This well planned city will now be gone under the sea. The huge city markets that held traders from all around the world will not be remembered in history. The northerly states that continuously traded with this city will have to search for another source for their weapons.

Lord Rama will be the last person to use the Brahmastra in this Yuga. He will be remembered as the ambassador for destroying evil, but this state which produced the Brahmastra will be eventually forgotten in history. All the people could do was pray.

Sanjay

#1

September, 2010
SBOA Matric School, Coimbatore

'Avanti can I have a word with you?' was all I could ask in the crowded cafeteria.

'What is it Sanjay?' she moved elegantly away from the counter with her food tray towards me. My gaze still stuck in those hazel eyes. The way her hair flutters when she walks.

I could still remember the first time I met this girl with an angelic smile. She came to me in one of those boring mathematics hours of our eleventh grade. I was busy solving the calculus problem that our faculty had given.

'Sanjay, could you help me with differential calculus?' I looked to see this new girl who had come to my school in the beginning of that month. She had joined here because her dad, who worked in a bank, got transferred. This new addition to our school had constant eyes and words floating around her. But she didn't seem to be bothered with anything other than this calculus problem.

'Sure, anything for the newcomer.' I said still unable to look away from her with an awkward smile. And that's how our friendship began. It has been a year since I solved that problem for her.

'Sanjay! Day dreaming already?' her shaking my shoulder brought me back to reality.

'What?' realizing what had happened 'Nothing!' I shook my head.

'What is that you want to ask me?'

'I don't know how to say it'

'Are you going to propose to me?' she burst out laughing.

I couldn't say a word. I hated myself for making it so obvious. But I had to say it. I never had enough guts to say it to her. But today I had made up my mind. I had rehearsed and prepared well on how to have this conversation. But this was unexpected.

'Yes Avanti, I love you.' I said it. My heart was racing like a cheetah. She became silent all of a sudden. She quietly got up from the table and walked out of the cafeteria. I didn't know whether I should follow her or stay quiet. I was waiting for something to happen. But nothing happened. Suddenly my phone vibrated. It was a text from her.

'u r my friend Sanjay. I can't love u.
Hope u understand.'

This is not what you want to hear from the girl whom you loved. I never approached her again nor did she speak. We were not meant to be together; at least that's what I thought.

#2

3 years later,
August, 2013
Amrita University.

'Geebi have you seen my assignments?' asked Kevin who was desperately searching the cupboards. 'I have to give it today to escape the wrath of Professor Ramesh'.

'Try checking my bag, I think I took it to copy the problems' said Geebi who was still lying in his bed. At that time, someone knocked on the door. 'Open the door you lazy goose' shouted Kevin who was turning everything out of Geebi's bag. Geebi murmured something and got out of his bed. If it was not for the Axe deodorant, Geebi wouldn't have known it was Rohit who was waiting outside the door. Rohit was the cool dude of the college. Ever since he came to Amrita, he had become the favourite among girls.

'Why so early man?' asked Geebi and let him in.

'Why else? To copy the assignment from Sanjay and Kevin' said Rohit, who came in his Volkswagen Polo. 'Of all the options out there, I still don't know why I took Aerospace engineering' blabbed Rohit as he entered the hostel room.

'Copy that!' Kevin threw the assignment which he had just now found from Geebi's bag. Rohit began copying the assignment busily. That's when I entered the room. 'Is the Axe machine here already?' I asked getting myself ready after the bath.

'Sanjay did you get the movie tickets?' Rohit tried to change the topic while his hand was busy writing.

'I am trying and it is not that difficult, we can manage it on the movie day.' I said. We packed our bags and left the hostel to our college. Me, Kevin and Geebi share a room in our college boys' hostel. Since our college was at a walkable distance from the hostel, Rohit parked his car in the hostel itself. On the way we met our friends from the girls' hostel.

'Hi guys' said Priya, with her big nerdy specs and huge volumes of books in her hands.

'Priya, please change the specs or I would have to call you Professor Priya' said Geebi and grabbed few books from her.

'I prefer the specs over contacts. It doesn't give me headaches' said Priya and letting him carry the books.

'And as usual Malvika and Avantika are coming late' said Rohit whose mobile beeped the message. Even though everything was over between me and Avantika, it makes me uncomfortable when she gets closer to Rohit. But I never bothered as long as I was with her. My thoughts were interrupted as I saw those beautiful hazel eyes again. She came with Malvika Menon.

'Sorry guys, held up there copying the assignment. Have you done it?' Avanti asked but her eyes were on Rohit. I didn't know what I could do, if she was interested in him. But I didn't want to be a burden to her after what had happened in school. She still speaks to me normally as if nothing had happened between us. She speaks and that's all that matters.

'Yes we copied too! Thanks to Sanjay and Kevin' said Rohit. Avanti smiled and our eyes met. Malvika directly went to Kevin and gave him a hug. They are a well-known couple in the college. It was a love at first sight for both of them in our first year. Since then, they had become the hot topic in our class. Kevin being the nicer and quiet person in the duo, always listens to her stories day and night. She on the other hand can talk for hours and hours without a break. Malvika was asking him on how she looked and if her lip gloss was proper and all those. We began walking towards the college.

Third year B. Tech Aerospace Engineering hall welcomed us. College was like as usual. Boring and long lectures, taking notes, presentations and assignments ruled most of our time. Today's lecture was on flight dynamics and control by Ms. Aydhika. She was in her mid-thirties and a fresh IIT masters' graduate.

'…. And that is how lateral stability is achieved.' She finished her long lecture. It was followed by Theory of Modern Avionics by Professor Ramesh. In the free time, we would hang out in the Dhaba outside our college. Food in the mess is not very satisfactory, so Krishna Dhaba is the only source of quality food outside the college.

'Are the tickets booked for *Chennai Express?*', asked Malvika, who was a hard-core fan of SRK.

'Sanjay says he has arranged the tickets.' said Rohit looking at me. I gave him an approving nod. Hot parathas and spicy curries filled our stomach. And we headed back to our college.

#3

'Why aren't the girls here?' I asked looking at my watch. It was 5 30. 'Only thirty minutes more for the movie.' Kevin was calling Malvika to ask where they were.

'They are on their way and will reach here in five minutes. But Avantika isn't coming.' said Kevin whose eyes were glued to the couple of girls who had just crossed us.

I interrupted him, 'Why isn't she coming?' His glance was still stuck on those girls. 'She is doing some broadcasting from her Ham radio.' he said. Avanti has been into this Ham radio from her second year in college, when her dad bought her a small Ham radio for her birthday. Ever since then, she has been regularly broadcasting her views, her opinions in her frequency. She even wrote an ASOC exam to get her frequency of operation. It became her electronic diary since then.

'Ok people you continue with the movie. I will go pick her up and come.' I suggested. When I was about to leave, 'Sanjay how are you planning to go?' asked Rohit.

'By bus' I said

'It will take ages for you to get there and you will come back only by the end of the movie. Let me bring my car.' he said. Only that seemed logical. And once again my hope of being with Avanti got screwed. 'See you guys' said Geebi with a large bucket of popcorn in his hand and went into the theatre.

* * * *

Avantika's home was in Race Course, one of the most posh areas in the city. After all the welcomes from her parents and answering all their questions about studies and everything, we finally went to meet her in her room. She was busy broadcasting something about development of our country and protecting environment. Her voice was booming everywhere in the room. She waved towards us and signalled that it would be over in five minutes.

'…. And today we are facing crisis because we have depleted all the non-renewable resources we had to sustain. But we still haven't reduced their consumption. Instead of going towards renewable energy, we still insist on borrowing non-renewable resources from other countries. It is time for us to wake up! Our ancestors knew about the ill effects of over-using the non-renewable resources. They even considered them as potential threats and hid the resources, deep inside forests…. If they were clever enough to save them, are we foolish enough to try and kill ourselves….' It went on and on. And then there were some questions from an old woman who had been listening to her program for long. Avanti replied to them patiently and thanked them for listening to her frequency.

'…. with that your loveable messenger Mercury is signing off. See you all next week.' Avantika turned down her Ham radio. She gulped down a whole glass of water.

'Mercury?' asked Rohit.

'Yes my radio name. Isn't it nice?'

'Yes but why? Avantika seems pretty neat!' Rohit exclaimed.

'Most people don't keep their real name in Ham. It is for safety' said Avanti. 'Hey Sanjay!' finally she looked at me. 'Aren't we late for the movie?'

'As a matter of fact, yes' I said.

'Then let us rush! I don't want to miss SRK' Avanti rushed us out of the house.

#4

Everyone seemed to be very busy with their work. What else can they do? Each professor was pressurizing the students to complete their course mini-project. There wasn't a conversation in the class without the words mini-project and presentations in them.

'I wish this semester gets over fast' said Kevin who got irritated with all the project work he had done yesterday.

'Yes and in the vacations, we will plan a big holiday to Kodaikanal' suggested Geebi.

'What about Munnar? Beautiful drive and the climate, it's just awesome' argued Malvika. Munnar was closer to her hometown.

'Guys I think that we should ask for a tour from the college.' said Kevin.

'Seem fair enough. We will ask our class reps to talk to our department head immediately' I said.

Next day there was a big meeting in the HOD's room. Representatives were arguing for a trip, while the faculties were countering them with poor performance in the internals. It went on for more than an hour. We were all gathered outside the room desperately waiting for a trip. We could hear Geebi along with the other class reps getting thrashed inside the HOD's room.

'I don't think we will get this trip.' said Nandita, one of our classmates.

The faith of getting a positive reply was now a distant hope. And finally they came out. Their faces showed otherwise.

'HOD has agreed for the trip' beamed Geebi. 'But the place will be selected by our HOD and it will be a three day trip' finished Yamini, the other representative. Everybody had a mixed joy. The notice came in a week.

To the students of third year Aerospace engineering,

As per your request, a recreational trip will be arranged for you. The place and details are given below. Interested students can register with your class counsellor by paying an amount of four thousand rupees by the evening of 30th September, 2013. Also attach a 'no objection certificate' from your parent/guardian.

No registration will be encouraged after the deadline.

Place   : Mundanthurai tiger reserve and Agasthya hills
Dates   : October 11th to October 14th

I hope you all enjoy the scenic beauty of the reserve forest without disturbing the Mother Nature. Professor Ramesh and Ms. Aydhika will be in charge for the trip.

Regards
Dr. Hemanth Chakrabarthi
Chairperson
Department of Aerospace

Many were happy that the trip was going to be a trekking trip. Few were unhappy that Professor Ramesh was accompanying us. And few more were scared that they may be eaten by some wild animals. But for us, it would be the most wonderful thing that is going to happen in this college life. Geebi was very happy because he always wanted a deep forest trekking trip. But Priya seemed to be the only person who was faking her smile. I approached her and asked her what had happened. 'I don't think I could come for the trip.' she said still continuing her fake smile.

'Why? Have you planned to study during that time?' I asked sarcastically.

'No Sanjay, it's just that my parents won't allow for such trips.' She continued, 'besides its four thousand bucks! You know my family situation right.' She said. I don't know what to reply to her. It's weird when we have this matured talk and think about all the family situations and problems. No reply seems appropriate. 'We will figure something out. And this will be the only trip of all of us together.' I said.

'I know, but try to understand. You guys enjoy. I have to return some books to the library, so see you soon' she vanished from my sight.

It was a cloudy Sunday in the hostel. The clouds were ready to pour out at any moment now. I told about the Priya issue to Rohit. Rohit suggested that he was ready to pay for her.

'But that will just create bitterness between her and her parents' Geebi said. It began to rain with mighty flashes and thunder. And the smell of the rain touching the soil was amazing.

'I would say that we should talk to her parents about this and convince them' I suggested.

'Ok let me get my car, we will pick the girls up and go to her house.' Rohit left to get his car. Kevin and Malvika were busy planning to go to a coffee shop in the evening. So we picked up Priya and Malvika from their hostel and headed for Priya's house.

'Where are we going?' Priya had asked. Rohit replied that we are headed to Fun Republic mall to do some shopping. Avantika never asked a question, when I said that Rohit asked her to join for shopping. She was just happy.

Priya's house was on the outskirts of the city, near Peelamedu. Her dad was a mill worker and her mother was a tailor. Their earnings were just sufficient for running the family. She joined the university, with a scholarship and her parents were happy about it. Being the only child, her parents never said no to her wishes. Whatever she asked, they got it even though it was out of their limit. But now she had become matured and realized her family situation. When we reached her house, she was shocked than surprised. Her house was decent, but small. From the outside we could see an old TVS 50 standing inside the half built compound wall.

'If it is for convincing my parents for the trip, then let's go back.' Priya said. 'I don't want to trouble them.' Avanti realized what was happening here, took Priya away from us and spoke to her. They started having the girls talk which went on for ten minutes. When she came she seemed composed. 'But if my parents say no, then that's it.' Priya said firmly.

We went and knocked on the door. Her mother welcomed us in. It was a nice house for a small family. Every corner of the house was either stacked with books or old newspapers. There weren't enough chairs inside the house, so Geebi said he would wait outside in the veranda. Her mom spread out a mat for all of us to sit and offered us coffee. We were not in a mood to drink coffee, so we politely declined the offer. She said Priya's father has gone for work.

Priya began to tell her mom about the trip. 'Before you say anything more Priya, listen to this latest news. Our HOD has informed the reps that for the top three rankers, the trip charges will be taken care by the institution.' Rohit said. Priya opened her mouth in shock, searching for words with her eyes protruding out.

'What? What trip is it Priya?' her mother asked.

'Amma it's a trekking trip to Mundanthurai forest.' She said.

'Isn't it dangerous? How did your college agree for it?' her mother started shooting questions.

'Aunty! It is not dangerous. Besides we are not going alone. Our faculty will be coming with us.' Avanti paused. 'It will be our last trip together aunty, please send her and also her expenses are taken care….' Avanti continued pleading with Priya's mom. I pretended that I got a call, and sneaked out of the house. I couldn't listen much to the girls talk! Rohit preferred to stay inside in order to keep his lie alive.

Geebi and I were waiting outside. He was throwing stones on the puddles formed in after the recent rain. From the puddle a huge frog jumped out, splashing water on him. 'I hate rains!' Geebi shouted. He was cleaning his pants with the small pot of water that was kept near the veranda.

'Do you think it will be raining during our trip?' I asked

'I hope it doesn't….' before he could complete the girls came out with Rohit. 'What happened? ' Geebi asked.

'Priya will be coming with us' beamed Avanti and hugged Priya.

'Awesome let us celebrate! Let's go to the Annapoorna!' suggested Geebi who was still cleaning the dirt on his pants. Priya's mom loaded us with a box full of sweets.

'Guys, drop me at my house. I have this Ham session by six!' Avanti said. Despite all of us forcing, Avanti wanted to stay back at home with her Ham. We had a quiet dinner at the Annapoorna.

#5

The rains have stopped. October came with a chilling breeze and less sunlight. In this lazy climate, getting up early and leaving for classes was the most difficult thing. Everyone was looking forward for the trip. Convincing my parents wasn't a big issue. They knew that the decisions I make are trust worthy. We had just one more week left for the trip. Many students didn't register for the trip, fearing that there won't be any enjoyment in the treks and rest fearing that they will catch some tropical disease. In the end around twenty eight of us registered for the trip.

Ms. Aydhika and Professor Ramesh came to our class and announced that there is a special meeting regarding the trip in the department's conference room after the classes. We were all eagerly gathered in the conference room by sharp four in the evening. Professor Ramesh and Ms. Aydhika came into the hall. Ms. Aydhika was in her usual sari with her hair tied in a bundle. We could never guess her age. It could be around forty or maybe even in the early thirties. But Professor Ramesh was very young and unmarried. He rose very quickly in the teaching ladder. When we were in our first year, he came to this college as a fresh M. Tech graduate from IIT. But he pursued his Ph. D. under our HOD, and completed it in less than three years. His tall and built physique makes him an eye catching specimen for all the young unmarried lady staffs. Ms. Aydhika drank some water and began,

'Good evening students. I hope all the twenty eight registered students are here.' Everyone nodded. 'Good. Then let us come to the plan. We will be leaving Coimbatore on 10th evening by train and reach Thirunelveli district the next day morning. From there we would head to the forest check post. There, we will have breakfast and proceed to the forest. You will be divided into four groups and each group will be headed by a forest guard. With the help of Govind Bhatt, I segregated you into four groups.' Geebi winked at us and said he has taken care of it. Geebi's original name is Govind Bhatt. We shortened by making it Geebi (GB). When she read out the group names, we realized why Geebi winked at us. He managed to keep all seven of us in the same group. There was some commotion in the crowd, not everyone was happy with the way the group was made. Ramesh silenced everyone and continued from where Ms. Aydhika left. 'From there we will head to Meakery village. And beyond the village, we will set a base camp in the banks of Thenarru River and stay for the night. Next day, we will trek alongside the Agasthya hills and reach Thaen aruvi. And on thirteenth, we will climb the pothigai peak and return to the base camp. From there we will leave for Coimbatore by night and reach here on fourteenth morning. Any questions?' asked Ramesh.

One of our over enthusiastic classmates Meera asked what all things they should bring. Miss Aydhika came forward and said, 'Everyone please have your hiking shoes, two bottles of water, high calorie snacks and chocolates, hand full of salt to avoid leeches and other basic necessities. Also learn the basics of tent construction.' We were imagining ourselves like Bear Grills from Discovery channel, climbing steep hills, walking through dense forest and living in tents hoping reality doesn't spoil our dreams.

We came to the Brookfields mall, to get some nice outfits to wear. Rohit and I went to shop for a decent torch light. The girls took this as a chance and went to the salon. Kevin and Geebi went to get some travel groceries. After that we headed back to the hostel.

#6

Never has the express train 16610 from Coimbatore to Thirunelveli come on time. And today was no different. We had been waiting for two hours and there was no sign of the train. Ms. Aydhika had been counting us every fifteen minutes to make sure everyone was there. Passengers were crawling through the gaps to get on to the general compartment of another train in platform number two. Geebi and Kevin went to Railway canteen to have their dose of dinner. Malvika was getting the air pillows for her and Kevin. Slowly the train approached the station with its bright lights in front of the engine into the platform number one. A sudden chill enveloped us. This was finally happening. We were really going for a trip. The berths were allotted based on our groups. So all seven of were in the same compartment.

As usual the compartments were infested with cockroaches and rodents. We were hesitant to keep our bags down. Moreover none of us were planning to sleep. So we arranged the entire luggage in the side upper berth and sat on the rest. It was going to be a long ten hour journey. We were playing cards, talking about everyone's school life, what we enjoyed the most in college. In the meantime Kevin and Rohit silently sneaked out of our coupe. That was not a good signal. It means they were planning to do something crazy.

Then came the time when everyone ran out of stories. The coupe became quiet. Chill wind was caressing our faces. Avanti pulled out her iPod and started listening to music. Geebi began checking out the new book he bought in the Higgin Bothams books store in the railway station. Priya and Malvika were looking into a laptop and giggling among themselves. I got up and went in search of those two.

I wouldn't have guessed that it was Kevin in this smoke, if it was not for his purple hoodie and the cross on his chest. He was sitting on the train's floor with Rohit and few other classmates, surrounded by many beer bottles and cigarette packets. The smoke was making me obnoxious. 'Come sit down bro! Grab a beer.' Rohit mumbled with all his strength. He was puffing the smoke from the cigarette. 'Nothing can ever come close to weed!' he said and letting the smoke evade out of the train. Everyone here was in a state of unconsciousness. Kevin was playing with the water leaking from the dirty washbasin. One more fellow named Gopal was shouting over the phone. That's when I saw Professor Ramesh coming from the other end of the compartment. Everyone started collecting the beer bottles and thrashing it outside the trains. Gopal ran into the toilet. Rohit and others got up and went to the next compartment. Kevin was unable to move and Ramesh caught us. Professor Ramesh came and looked around. Kevin was leaning over, struggling to stand straight. I thought this was the end of our trip. But Ramesh sir came and took Kevin's other hand over his shoulders. I became speechless and produced a fake smile. Looking at my confused face, he said 'I too have crossed your age. But keep it within limit.' He smiled.

The beautiful city of Thirunelveli welcomed us in the morning. The lush green trees and the scent of lily flowers on the ladies' hair overwhelmed our senses. The sky was overcast. Porters were barging into the train to help us with our luggage. The railway station was crowded with the busy daily vendors selling their farm vegetables and fruits. The workers were trying to nudge through the vendors to catch the local trains for reaching their work.

Eventually everyone managed to get out of the station. We were supposed to be travelling in a bus arranged by the District Forest Office. It was not a luxurious bus. The seats weren't proper and were shaking throughout the whole journey. The road to Meakery village was shadowed by trees either sides. Grey clouds and cool breeze were already making us like this place. As we moved away from the city, houses became fewer and more foliage were covering both the sides of the road.

The bus stopped in the forest check post. The road ahead could not be traversed by the bus. We got down from the bus and headed to the check post. It was a small building, raised on the ground, with just two rooms. It had a faded board reading Thirunelveli Forest Check Post hanging from top.

Professor Ramesh went and spoke to a person. Just from the first look we could say that he was the incharge of this place. He was in his khaki uniform and boots. If I would have to guess his age, it would have been around forty. He shook his muscular hands with Professor Ramesh and Ms. Aydhika. They were talking for few minutes and into his walkie-talkie the muscular man said something. About five jeeps came to the check post barricade from behind the building. People were already updating their Facebook status about their visit to this forest.

#7

From the jeep near the barricade came out a person, who seemed odd when compared to the rest of the other forest guards. His lean unfit body with unshaved beard made him an odd man out in the collection of guards.

'I bet he has a lost love story!' said Geebi looking at him. I thought whether I should grow more beard and searched for Avanti. But she was having tea with Rohit in the small petti shop. Much time had passed by and I guessed I had to move on. Ms. Aydhika called out to everyone to come around the entrance of the check post building. She stood on the veranda and began announcing. 'In another fifteen minutes we will start from here to Meakery village. Mr. Anand and his team will be taking care of us from now.' She said and let Anand speak. He thanked her and started speaking. 'I hope you all had a good night's sleep in the train. Because I bet next three days, no one will think about sleep.'

Everyone shouted in excitement. He continued, 'But bear this in mind, you are going to a village that is far from city standards. You won't get a sophisticated villa for your stay. You won't get various cuisines for your food. There won't be any electronic support inside the reserve forest.' Everyone's faced turned dull. 'But I can assure you that you will see a whole new world inside the forest. From wild animals to beautiful rivers to mesmerizing sunset, everything will bring a new perspecive in your life.' Everyone was dumbstruck on what Anand has said. The sky was turning bright and birds started to chirp in search of their morning prey. 'So let us start from here. It will take an hour's journey from here. I suggest you all have your morning coffee or tea from the petti shop.' He finished.

Everyone was busily having their morning refreshments from the petti shop. The old man in the shop was having difficulties in serving a large crowd like this. The radio in the shop was playing a song from the film Roja. AR Rahman's first movie which got him introduced to the world of cinema.

> *'chinna chinna aasai, siraga adika aasai,*
> *muthu muthu aasai, mudinthu kolla aasai,*
> *vennilavai thotu muthamida aasai,*
> *ennai intha boomi sutri vara aasai.'*

Priya was humming Vairamuthu's lyrics from the radio. Geebi, a great lover of coffee, was gulping down his third cup to stay awake in this cloudy morning. Around seven, Anand and four other guards collected their group of students and went to their jeep. The whole journey was very bumpy. The pathway wasn't meant for travel by any vehicle. It was a mud path carved for transporting camp elephants from the village. The influence of the forest instantly struck us. The smell of the fresh pine and eucalyptus diffused through the air and hit our senses. There was unusual quietness in the surroundings except for the monkeys crisscrossing the jungle paths in search of their morning food.

Priya took out her film camera and started taking pictures. Our mobile phone's network ran out.

'I already love this place.' Kevin said. 'That's it. I am going to become a forest ranger and settle in a place like this.' Everyone was spellbound throughout the journey. Finally a board reading 'Meakery gramam' was seen. A few thatched roofs were seen at a distance. The ploughed fields replaced the towering trees. People were eagerly getting into the fields to do their routine work. We stopped in front of a brick building. Anand and Ramesh went inside the building. In the meantime, another guard named Mohan asked us to follow him for the breakfast, while Anand and faculties finished the procedures. We were escorted by the other four guards, out of which Mohan was the only one not in khaki uniform.

In the open lands behind the brick building, the villagers had pitched a huge marquee for our temporary stay and breakfast. At one end, there was a fire pit for cooking. Few unusually shaped vessels were placed over the pit. There was a mud pot which was closed at the top, but had a hole by its side. An old lady in white sari with her head covered with the sari was mixing something with a stick in the mud pot. Few other ladies similarly dressed were working over the fire pit. There were not any chairs for us to sit. We sat on the ground. Children from village had come up to serve us food.

They laid a big banana leaf in front of everyone. We were quite used to this as it was common in several South Indian weddings. But Malvika was new to this. She did not want to get herself dirty by sitting on the mud floor. 'Ewww…. How can you sit and have food in such dirty place!' Malvika sprinted outside the marquee. Kevin went behind her.

'I hope she gets used to this. I don't think we will get any luxury in the entire trip' I said.

'We cannot blame her too. She was brought up in that way. She complains about the standards of our college every day to her dad.' said Avanti.

Kevin came back. 'She definitely needs to change her attitude.' He was angry with her.

'Is she going to eat something?' Priya asked.

'She is sitting in front of that brick building and having some biscuits I got.' Kevin sat in front of an unoccupied banana leaf. One by one the kids started placing items on the leaf. There were many items which we never knew about.

Priya pulled one girl and asked 'Hey what is this dish called?' in Tamil. The ten year old girl explained about all the dishes. A dish which looked like parathas, tasted sweet. Later we came to know from the girl that its name was Thuppidittu which had its origin from Badaga clan from the Nilgiris. There was also a dosa which was made in wheat and a curry with beans.

After we ate, we took the leaf and dropped in an open pit outside the marquee. The breakfast was heavy. Anand came and announced that we would be leaving in fifteen minutes and asked us to get ready. Suddenly Mohan came with a walkie-talkie and gave it to Anand. He walked away from us and spoke into it. His face suddenly became gloomy and turned red. After the call Anand said something to Mohan. Mohan immediately left with one other guard in a jeep.

Everyone was anxious to know what had happened. Anand sensing the anxiety said, 'I don't think we will leave early. There has been an issue.' He said. We all stared blankly hoping to get more information on the recent issue. He continued, 'A male Asian tusker was spotted near the area where you are going to camp. I have sent Mohan to check the place. Once he comes back, we can proceed.' Ms. Aydhika and Mr. Ramesh joined us.

'This is why I said that people were not allowed during restricted months. But your college officials insisted with to the District Forest Officer and we couldn't say no.' Anand said to Ramesh. Ramesh tried to speak, but he backed out. We were ever more excited than before. More than the fact that our HOD had struggled to get this trip, the possibility of an elephant in our camp site captured all our imaginations.

Now that we had a lot of time left, we planned to roam around the village. Priya found the small girl who served us food and asked her to show us around. Kevin and Malvika were planning to go around on their own and spend some time alone. More than that Malvika was not comfortable with the village atmosphere. Rohit excused himself to go and get the binoculars from the jeep.

So Geebi, Avantika and I followed the kid with Priya. The kid was comfortable talking to Priya as she spoke Tamil very well.

'What is your name darling?' she asked in Tamil.

'Veera' she said.

'Which class are you studying?'

'I don't go to school *akka*!' she said. 'Why?' Priya's face turned dull.

'We don't have a school. The closest one is near the check post. On the way you saw the check post right?' We all nodded. Even though they had changed a lot from their ancestors, formal education was not easily available to them.

Veera took us around the place where her house was. The house had a big open space in the front. It was meant for the cattle, goats and other farm animals. In her house, they had a large number of goats.

The houses were constructed with clay and mud. Her house was simple and identical to its neighbours. There was not any separate fencing between the goat's shed and the pavement to her house. The goats bleated and started running around, seeing us intruding into their territory. Geebi got stuck between the herd and screamed. Especially the one with the bell around its neck seems to be very angry with Geebi's actions.

Veera laughed and went towards the herd, 'Mani!' she called out to the goat with the bell. She lifted the goat and helped Geebi get out of the herd.

'This is Mani! My pet!' Veera said.

'It's so cute!' exclaimed Avantika. She started playing with its foot.

'How old is it?' I asked. Priya was taking pictures of this young goat.

'He is just one year old' Veera said. Geebi was staying away from form us, especially from Mani.

'Fold your hands, I will give you water to drink' Veera said on seeing Geebi gasping after his adventure with the goats.

'Fold my hands?' Geebi questioned and folded his hands as a sign of respect.

'Ayyo anna not like that' she folded Geebi's hands and made his palm like a cup. From the mud pot, she poured water and asked him to drink.

'What like this? Isn't there a cup or tumbler?'

'No! Your hands are like cups. If you want, drink. I can't hold the pot anymore!' she said and kept the pot down. Geebi tried his level best to hold both his palm together and drank the water.

Hearing all this commotion, a lady came out. Her appearance shocked us. She covered most of her body with the sari she wore. But she couldn't hide it completely. The skin was swollen and wrinkled all over her hands and face. Her left eye was becoming nearly invisible, covered by her own aging skin that hung out. The ears had become dislocated on both the sides. Same was the case with her hands. She was seriously affected by some skin disease. We couldn't say a word on seeing that. Veera's cute face suddenly expressed a sense of shock and guilt.

'Ma, why did you come out?' she asked in Tamil.

'I heard some noise, thought you might be in ...' the lady replied in her squeaky voice.

'Didn't you hear what the Ranger said?'

'Yes...' she breathed silently and went inside. Veera was still staring at the place where the lady had stood. Priya went closer and placed her hand over Veera's shoulder. Little drops of tears rolled down her cheeks and fell on Priya's hand.

'That… That is my mother' Veera said. 'She was not like this before.' Priya pulled her into a hug. Veera said that her parents and many other people had been working in the forest stone quarry to get construction stones for our village. After some months her father fell ill like her mother and died. For getting little more money her mother joined work. She also said that around seven people have already died and many are in her mother's condition.

'Did you not visit any hospital?' Avanti asked.

'No, we don't have any hospital close by. The nearest one is in Ambasamudhiram.' She said.

'We had a doctor coming and checking on every month. But now he has stopped coming saying that the disease may be contagious and there is no cure for it.

Geebi was about to say something but he stopped. 'Come, I will take you to the temple.' Veera said. Geebi managed to get out of the herd very quickly. The temple was in far end of the village. It was dedicated to Rain God. The temple looked abandoned and was locked.

'Why is the temple locked?' I asked.

'It closes for three months every year. That too during the rainy season' Veera said.

'Do you know why?' Geebi asked.

'My grandmother told me a story long ago. There was a king who ruled the coastal land several thousands of years ago. He abandoned his kingdom for unknown reason and came to this place and built a new city. At that time he built this temple. And for three months in a year, he would sit and pray inside this temple for forgiveness. He did not like to be disturbed; hence the guards locked him inside the temple for those three months. We still believe that the king comes and prays during these three months. That why we locked it.' Veera finished.

'I never heard of such a king in the history books' Geebi said. A girl of Veera's age ran and came towards us. She told that Ranger Anand was waiting for us. We said bye to Veera. Avanti and Priya hugged her and asked her not to worry.

Veera had got Priya a present. 'It's a goat. I made it myself with clay.' She said and gave it to her. Priya thanked her and kissed her goodbye.

#8

Everyone gathered around the brick building. Kevin and Malvika were in their own world. 'Is everyone here?' asked Ms. Aydhika, who again started counting us. 'Maybe one day she will get bored.' I thought. In the far end we could see a person sitting in the front seat of jeep. And Mohan was holding his legs and was wrapping a long cloth around his leg. He seemed to be in an excruciating pain. We were familiar with that person who had aviators over his collar and that physique.

'Oh my God! Rohit is hurt' Avanti screamed. I didn't realize that even she was looking at the same. Avanti sprinted towards him. We followed.

'Rohit... Rohit... what happened?' Avanti struggled for words.

'Chill Avanti! Just got my ankle sprained.' Avanti stood shaking at the spot.

'Where did you go bro?' asked Kevin.

'I was checking out the forest and thought of taking a small hike' he winked. 'and tripped over a banyan tree root.'

'Luckily I was around there. I brought him back' said Mohan. He finished wrapping the crepe band around his leg. 'Now try walking.'

Rohit got up and started limping and was struggling to walk. I went over and supported his left shoulder and Kevin took his right. And we slowly marched to the brick building and joined the group. Anand was explaining about the use of emergency flares and construction of tent. Mohan approached Anand and signalled him to come down the platform. Anand let another guard to take over and came down to Mohan. Mohan explained about the incident. Anand came to Rohit. On seeing Anand, Ramesh sir and Ms. Aydhika joined us.

'Can you walk now?' he asked Rohit.

'I can! Just need some rest.' Rohit struggled to get up. Anand insisted that he sit. Ms. Aydhika and Ramesh listened to whole incident from Mohan. And the worst we feared happened.

'I suggest we take him to a hospital' suggested Ms. Aydhika.

'There is no good hospital around here' said Priya recalling Veera's words. Anand nodded in agreement.

'We can probably take him to a hospital in the Thirunelveli city or if he can bear the pain, we can send him back home.' Ramesh sir said.

'No… no… sir. I can manage. It is not a big deal.' Rohit again struggled to get up from the place. He rejected Kevin's help to stand up and got up on his own.

'Sir please don't send me back. I have been waiting for this trip for a long time. I don't want to miss all the fun.' Rohit pleaded. The guard's instruction was echoing in the back.

'But in this state…'Ramesh began.

'He is coming!' finished Anand. 'If he is ready to come, then it's his wish' Anand said and patted Rohit's back. The other guard had finished the instructions and was waiting for Anand's approval. Anand went on the platform.

'Are we all ready?' Anand asked.

'YES!' everyone shouted in unison.

'OK before we start, every group will receive a map from the guards.' He gave a sign to the guards to distribute the maps.

'Now this map is in case you get lost somewhere in the forest. And let's all hope that doesn't happen. Anand gave a stern look at Rohit. Rohit nodded. We helped the guards unload all the essentials from jeep-the emergency flares, ropes food and fruits. Geebi was talking to the guards and Ramesh sir. The tarpaulin tent was tempting us to get inside. For most of us, this was the first hiking trip. There were a few who were professional trekkers and campers but in the other groups. They had worked with NGO's and government for forest animal census and other activities. For us seven, this was a dream come true.

'Guys, guess who will be our guard in charge?' Geebi asked.

'Don't say it is Anand sir himself!' said Priya.

'It is!' beamed Geebi. Anand sir was coming toward us.

'I guess I am stuck with you people for more time' he said. 'I hope you don't mind?' he asked and went near Rohit. He was sitting under the shade of a tree.

'It's an honour sir.' Rohit said. We all nodded. Geebi explained about the achievements of Anand. He was from the same Meakery village and had to travel for about 15 kilometres every day for his school. Then he went for training in Dehra Dun and got posting over here as forest ranger. We truly felt that we were lucky to have him as our guide.

The base camp was down the slope, behind the village temple. We left the village and headed down the slope. The pathway was treacherous. Even though there wasn't much height to descend, carrying all those supplies made the journey exhausting. Once we reached the plains, it was like travelling through a maze. There were thorny shrubs hindering our path. Guards had to cut these branches to let us through.

'Did you hear that?' Geebi said.

'Hear … hear what?' Malvika asked.

'The soothing sound of flowing water!' The silent rolling of water was slowly piercing behind the chopping of the thorny branches. The sound was getting louder and louder. A few moments later, we could see the small river crossing our path from left to right.

'This is where we will spend our night' Anand announced.

Every one of us dropped our supplies and ran towards the river. Only when we went closer, we realized that the water was not very deep. We ran into the river to pour out all our exhaustion. A sudden chill ran through us. All our pants became wet and heavy. Ms Aydhika asked us to come out.

'Don't worry ma'am. It is not very deep and there is no current.' Anand once again saved us from the clutches of our professors. He had always been friendly towards us. We splashed water on each other, played, ran in the water as if there was no end to it.

'Had enough fun?' asked Anand. We gave a weak yes.

'When will the food be served?' asked Malvika.

'There won't be any serving business Madam! We have to cook our own food here.' said Anand.

'What?' said Malvika sounding shocked and went away with her earpods. We were hoping that the sun would shine to dry our pants. It was like a heavy weight had been tied on our legs.

'Everyone gather around!' Ramesh shouted.

Anand began, 'Before we cook our lunch, we have to pitch a plane for our stay.' Once again everyone was happy.

'Now it is easily said than done. Each team has to fetch their own poles and corner stone for the tent.'

There was blankness in everyone's eyes. We hoped that we would be helped in the whole process.

'What are you waiting for? Get working. You have one hour.' Anand finished.

With an axe in hand, Geebi and I went in search for poles for our tents. Rohit went to fetch stones and Avanti joined him. Priya and the couple were looking for a nice spot for our tent. It was very difficult to find a long straight pole in the short thorny shrubs. And the ones which were long were shrouded with branches that broke while trimming them.

We were worn out when we returned to the camp site. The muscular Rohit and Kevin were hammering the tent's leg into the ground. Thud... thud… the noise was echoing all around the camp site. It was amazing to see the first construction that we put together.

Lunch was nothing but noodles and some boiled vegetables. It was difficult convincing Malvika to adjust with the limited resources. Being the only daughter of a big business magnet from Kerala, she was never denied anything. From the day she opened her eyes, she had the nest of everything. In her early years when both her parents were partners in a booming market foundation, Malvika had at least two servants taking care of her needs. But what she needed was love and affection, not uncared services.

In school, she became a spoilt brat. Education was not a problem for her. But it was the influence of other business giant's children, who introduced her to the other side of this calm world.

#9

'Are you serious?' Avanti asked, 'Are you the white tiger?' she was yet to come out of shock.

'Yes that's how I am called' said Mohan raising his eyebrows a little.

'I'm a huge fan of yours! I never miss your Friday 5pm talk. I even postponed my talk to 5:30 so that I could listen to yours!'

'Are you a HAMer? Rohit didn't tell me that' Mohan was looking at Rohit. We were outside our tents having hot tea and fresh fruits. Avanti blushed and nodded.

'So how many followers do you have Avanti?' Mohan asked.

'Very few. Around five to ten.' her face turned sad.

'That too grandmas and grandpas!' Rohit laughed hard. Avanti gave him a slight punch.

'That's nice. For a beginner, that's admirable' Mohan said. Avanti put up that slight smile over her lips.

'Avantika, do you want to see my instrument?' Mohan asked.

'Is it possible?' Avanti was dumbstruck.

'That's not a problem! But the only thing is we have to come back before seven. We have an elephant corridor on the way!' Mohan explained about the recent sightings of the elephants near the village and how it had dreadfully attacked an old man.

'That's not a problem! Let's start now' Avanti was very enthusiastic. Mohan spoke to Anand and came back with a backpack. Avanti got ready very quickly. I gave her a bottle of water. She smiled.

'Do you want to come with us?' she asked. Never knew just a few words could give goosebumps, that too from someone special.

'Did you ask Rohit?' I asked. But I knew the answer beforehand.

'Yes. But he couldn't come because of his leg.' She put up that long sad face.

'Yes!' I said just for the sake of being her company. We traced back the same route uphill to the village. The mighty sun was slowly sinking behind the Western Ghats. The village was lit with glowing fire from burning wood. Street lights were out of question when the village was even deprived of electricity. We had our torch lights to show us the way. There was an unusual sound of wailing heard.

'What is that Mohan?' I asked. The sound was a mix of conch and bells in some rhythmic fashion. I could guess what it could be. Deaths always lead us to pains even if the person is not known to us.

He asked a passer-by. 'A lady passed away' the passer-by said.

'Is it because of some unknown radiation?' Avanti asked.

'Radiation? What radiation?' Mohan was anxious.

'The radiation from some mine or something' she said.

'No…no … there isn't anything like that! She died because of some flu she caught in our village' he said coldly. 'Poor Veera what is she going to do? Both her parents…' he murmured.

'The lady was Veera's mother? I asked

'Yes. You know her?' he asked. I nodded and still couldn't believe what I heard. We just met her in the morning and now she is gone. Fate plays unfair tricks on good people I thought.

'I think we should get going there isn't much time left' Mohan tapped on his watch.

'Avanti go with him. I will go check on Veera.' I said. Avanti said she too wanted to come. 'No! He took pains to come this far. Go with him and don't miss the Ham.' I paused. She was not convinced. 'And it won't be nice if many of us show up there.' This time I won over her. She nodded and left with Mohan.

It was not difficult to find Veera's house. So many villagers were gathered outside her house. The goats have been moved to the neighbouring fields. The whole village was there mourning over the lifeless body. My eyes searched for Veera. She was sitting near the steps where Geebi drank the pot's water. She stayed there motionless, unable to believe that her mother was no more. Her hand was cuddling her pet goat Mani. The loss of her mother was irreplaceable. I could only imagine how she would have enjoyed the company of her mother. Her mother catching the wild disease would have affected her very much. Now that had left her with no family.

I was feeling as though I lost someone close to me. I hardly knew this child. But her smile had made an ever lasting impression on me. People, one by one went and placed rice into her mouth. A small fire was lit up. Priests began their rituals and Veera just did as she was instructed. The village men carried her mother to the final resting.

'This is the eighth person' someone said in Tamil.

'I don't know how much more we have to take this to come back to a peaceful life.' Another one said.

Veera looked at me. Her eyes said how she was feeling. The red eyes had exhausted all the tears it had. I felt a hand over my shoulder.

Avanti was pressing my shoulder and crying. She went straight to Veera to console her. 'She didn't even listen to what I explained about HAM! Is she really into HAM?' Mohan asked. I guess he was really frustrated over us. After all coming so far was of no use.

'Yes she is. But I guess this had disturbed her' I said pointing to the procession that was leaving the house.

'Does she know them already? Are they related?' he asked once again.

'No ... no... we met them today morning only' I said.

'We should get going. It's already late', he said.

We couldn't have dinner properly. It was pricking my throat. Geebi had been consoling Priya from the moment we broke the news to her and everyone else. From the camp site we could see the light from the village. I was thinking what Veera would be doing now. First day of our trip ended on a sad note.

#10

'Why can't she come with us?' Priya said at the top of her voice. It was still dark outside and Geebi was waking every one of us.

'What time is it?' Kevin asked.

'It's 5 already, we have to start early! Go get ready.' Geebi said. 'And don't forget there is no special place as toilet. It's all done in the open.' I was shocked.

'Yes and do it before the sun rises if you don't want anyone to notice' Geebi said. There was no other reason required than this. We got out of our tent in God speed.

'Why is Priya shouting out there?' asked Rohit, who came out of that small door of our tent.

'Oh that' Geebi paused, 'She wanted to bring that small girl Veera with us for the trek.'

'And?' I asked.

'And our faculties as usual are not agreeing to it.' Geebi finished. We went closer to the small gathered crowd to know more.

'…what will she do alone? And what is it going to cost? She is just a small girl.'

'Priya don't involve in unnecessary things. Go get ready. We have a long trek ahead!' said Ramesh Sir.

'This is not unnecessary. It's just a small help we can do.'

'There is nothing wrong in what you said but we are not here for this.' Ramesh sir said. Anand came to see the gathered crowd.

'If it's the cost that you are worrying about, I am ready to spend for her. It is not new to me.' Rohit said realizing how he made Priya believe that the college paid for her trip. Even in this gloomy early morning Priya's face expressed the questioning look on what Rohit said. Realizing the situation, Anand said

'I am really happy Ms. Priya on seeing your courage and boldness. Your social interest is indeed remarkable.' He said. 'But don't you think we should ask Veera first about it. And also more than that there are rituals and offerings that has to be followed in our village, if a soul leaves the body.' He stopped. Anand was staring at Malvika. Her ears were plugged with her earphones. 'You city dwellers might have forgotten what our culture and heritage means.' He turned towards Priya and said. 'Let's not change that, shall we?' he smiled. Priya too nodded.

We finished our morning chores and dismantled our tent. Hot toast and boiled eggs were made for breakfast.

We headed towards the Thenarru River. The trek had a beauty of its own. To our left there were huge hills, which were never endingly long, followed us throughout our way. The sun was blessing us with its early morning rays. Priya was still upset that we couldn't bring Veera with us.

'Sir, I am really sorry for the trouble I caused.' said Avanti.

'That's never a problem' replied Mohan with a smile.

We took rest at the banks of Sittraru river. The water here was much clearer than the water in the Thenarru River. We refilled our water bottles and continued our journey. The water was just knee deep and cold. The clouds cleared letting the scorching sun heat us. In no time the bottles drained down. We headed into the Agasthya hills. The small path was making our journey difficult. Above that the scorching sun made us literally bathe in our own sweat.

Down the hill, it was a better journey. The trees provided us the much needed shade. There wasn't much food to munch on, except the green cucumber and carrots. We were desperately hoping to see the honey falls soon. But the dense forest kept it hidden.

'Do you have anything else to eat?' Geebi asked the guard. He gave him two more cucumbers.

'No thanks, I am getting more and more allergic to these cucumbers.' Geebi said.

Kevin and Rohit had disappeared in other groups. I bet they were trying to light up their smoke. It was then we saw that. Cutting through the tall mountains of Suri hills from the very top, water was throttling down with a thunderous sound. It was one of those sights for which you wished you had more than two eyes. It was the honey falls.

#11

It was the place where the angels from heaven came for cleansing themselves. The pool formed at the bottom was huge as it could get. Small rocks protruding from the pool had small plants growing on them. The sparkling clear water, untouched by any human, caressing the small plants and fishes under it, the river Thenarru begins its journey here.

'Look at the rainbow over the falls.' beamed Malvika. It was the first time in whole trip Malvika seemed to be happy. Priya started taking pictures in her old fashioned roll camera that never left her.

This time before anyone jumped into the water, Anand gave his instructions 'Students you have the whole day left for you to spend at this falls. But before getting inside, let's pitch up the tent and get our dinner ready.'

'Not again!' grieved Manoj, one of our classmates.

'I am afraid there is no other way my friend' said Anand. Rohit was feeling better now as his limbs were in proper form. Rohit and I had collected some dry wood to make fire. Since the monsoon had started, it was difficult to get dry wood. And the mercury will lay low during the nights. Malvika was mesmerized by the beauty of the falls. She had gone into the water while others were working. Following her many had dived into the sparkling water.

Our tent took shape. And the smell of hot Maggie and boiled vegetables were creating grumbling noise of our intestinal juices. Many people had gone near the falls where the water was falling with an enormous force.

'Dude, that girl went inside water and never came up.' I said.

'Oh that girl Veena is an excellent swimmer. She might be doing some deep water swimming. Come help me with this' Rohit said lifting one side of the log. I lifted the other end and searched where she had surfaced. She didn't. Malvika and Kevin were happily playing with the water.

'Will you be ever like them?' I asked him pointing at them.

'I haven't found anyone yet and...' Rohit dropped the log and sprang into the water.

'Aaah! That hurts!' feeling a heavy thud on my leg. I moved the log and searched where he was going in a hurry. Seeing Rohit jump Avanti came to the rocky side of the reservoir. She held out her hand to pull her up. I helped her to get place. She was holding my hand for balance. I let her hold. He took a deep breath and went inside the water. She tightened her grip. 'Where is he going?' she asked. My eyes were transfixed on her hand over mine. I was in a different dimension. Realizing that I am not responding, she caught me looking at her hand. Immediately she took her hand away.

'Oh… he didn't say' I said realizing how stupid I was. Finally he came out. But there was something over his shoulder. It was a person. He was struggling to swim back with a person to hold. Kevin pulled Veena from Rohit and helped him get back to shore. She was still unconscious. Rohit was pressing her abdomen to spill out water from her lungs. She wasn't breathing still.

'Call Anand… call Aydhika Mam' Rohit was shouting. They were far from shore, near the tents. Two of our classmates went to call them. There wasn't any sign of movement from Veena. She was lying there motionless. I didn't know what was running in Rohit's mind, he placed his mouth over Veena's mouth to make her breathe. Avanti's eyes were wet with tears, she moved away from the crowd. Veena let out a heavy cough and spat all the water out of her body. Everyone was joyously hugging and patting Rohit for his brave effort. Veena was carried back to the tent.

'Sorry about the log Sanjay!' Rohit said.

'Don't worry about it.' I hesitated. 'I think you should talk to Avanti.'

'What happened?' he asked.

'Just talk to her…' it was really hard to say those words. But her happiness came before my love. Always.

Anand had strictly instructed that no one should enter into the waters again. Dinner was nothing special. But the camp fire was. Many unusual things were happening. Ramesh sir was dancing; Ms. Aydhika was eccentric with her song. But what caught the attention of everyone was this.

'Will you dance with me?' Rohit asked Avanti. She said yes without wasting even a second.

They were elegant with their steps. The song that was sung by everyone did not suit with the steps they were portraying. Her hand was running around his waist.

'Whoa oh! I didn't see that coming' Kevin said and jumped in the centre with Malvika. The teachers were shocked to see all this but didn't say anything. If it wasn't for the glare from the fire lit at the centre, Priya wouldn't have noticed the tears trickling down my eyes. She produced a fake smile in her face and murmured 'It's ok.' I left early to sleep.

*　　*　　*　　*

Anand came into the tent. We were getting ready for the morning trek to Pothigai peak. It was the last day of the trip. Everyone was sad that the trip was getting over.

'Can I have a word with you Rohit?' he said.

'Sure sir! Any problem?' Rohit asked.

'How is your leg now? Feeling better?'

'Yes sir I am perfectly alright.'

'The thing is Pothigai peak is a steep climb.'

'That's not a problem sir! I can climb even the Himalayas right now.'

'I appreciate the confidence. But it is not what you imagine it to be...' he paused. 'I suggest you to stay out of this trek and take rest.' That was it. There was no one to question Anand. Rohit was staying back. Malvika voluntarily backed out from this. She was much worried about her skin tan. Ms.

Aydhika, Veena, Gopal and few others too decided to spend their time over the falls.

'Can I talk to him?' Avanti asked Rohit.

'No… that's ok. I am bit tired actually. You have fun out there.' Rohit said.

'Ok.'

'And stay safe.'

'Hmm..'

'Avanti…' Rohit paused. Avanti looked at him. 'You are a good dancer. You were excellent yesterday.' Avanti blushed. Her cheeks turned red. I still didn't know why I was seeing and listening to this conversation.

'I am going to miss you.' Avanti put up a sad face.

'I will see you soon. Now go and have fun.'

Rohit hugged her. I turned and walked away. It is hard to see your girl with another guy and its worst to see her with your best friend.

Avanti was sad the whole journey. The trek to Podigai peak was indeed difficult. But the view from the top was majestic. We could see lush green serene forest till the horizon.

'Hey see Thaen aruvi' screamed Priya.

'Wow. Guys let's take a picture here.' Geebi said. 'Priya if you would do the honour.'

Priya took some wonderful pictures of us. It was a wonderful place. Only person who was unhappy was Avanti.

'Do you really miss him?' I asked.

'Yes.' She said.

'Hmm..'

'I am sorry'

'For what?' I asked.

'I know that you liked me and ...'

'Never mind forget it' I put up a smile. 'Did you tell him?'

'No.... not yet.... it is difficult to look at his eyes and....'
she caught me looking at her beautiful hazel eyes.

'Sanjay you have to move on' she said. The birds were
flying back to their nests.

'I have.... seriously moved on' I said.

'Don't lie to me. I have been noticing you'

'Noticing me for what?' Priya came to have a picture
with Avanti.

'Nevermind' she said and left.

*   *   *   *

'Did he say anything before leaving' I asked.

'He just said he will get some mangoes and left.' Malvika
said.

'Which way did he go?' Anand asked. Malvika pointed
to the direction we came.

'That leads us to the base camp. Anyway Mohan take
one more guard with you.' Mohan nodded. 'Call back in
53.4' He raised his walkie talkie and left. There was a heated
discussion between Anand and Ramesh sir. Anand came
to Aydhika Mam. 'How long did you say he was missing?'

'Its five hours now. I shouldn't have let him go.' Ms.
Aydhika started weeping.

'That's okay. He would have lost track of the way.'
Anand said. 'We will find him.' He called our group and
asked if we had known anything. We didn't know anything
and we won't be playing on things like this.

'Is it one of those pranks?' roared Ramesh sir. 'If I find
out anything like that, I will make sure you get suspended.'

'Chill Professor. They are not responsible for it. Let's find him first.' Anand said. 'What time did you say your train is?'

'Early morning 4:30' Ramesh said.

'I would suggest you all should start heading back to the village. The jeeps will take you back to the railway station.' Anand said.

'But Rohit?' Geebi asked.

'Our whole team is searching for him. We will find him and bring him before dawn' he assured.

'Sir let me stay back and help in your search' Avanti said.

'Me too...' I said. And Kevin and Geebi nodded.

'No let's not risk everyone's life. Beside it's getting dark and we don't have enough resources, if there is a wildlife encounter.' Anand said. We were hoping that Rohit would have gone ahead to reach the village. But there was another thought running over everyone's mind. No one dared to speak it out. Hope he never had to encounter the wild animals alone.

#12

Ramesh sir still thought that we were behind Rohit's missing. Geebi was explaining that we were not at all involved.

'Sir, he is our friend. More than anyone, we want him back with us. Besides that we don't know what trouble he got into.' Kevin stormed into Ramesh sir and held his shirt. Geebi pulled him back. Malvika was shocked on seeing Kevin this ferocious. We can't blame her. Girls weren't taken to gang fights or the breakouts that happen in hostel. Being from Christian missionary, Kevin has been or lived in a house of parents, cousins or grandparents. To him, everything is his friends. It took him long time to get close to us, but after that he is inseparable.

Ramesh sir was yet to come out of the shock. Maybe this was the first time, somebody had held him by his collar.

'Instead of questioning us, let's help the guards in finding Rohit' Avanti was shouting in her full voice. Kevin evaded from Geebi's grip and went back inside the tent. Everyone was looking at Ramesh sir. Geebi was asking for his forgiveness for what Kevin had done. Sir didn't even react to what Geebi said. He looked around at everyone and went back to his tent. It was a very chaotic situation. On one side Mohan and other guards were trying to find Rohit, and on the other side Ramesh sir had muted himself to whatever we said. Out pots didn't brew Maggie that night. No one felt the urge to eat. We didn't want to be here. We wanted to go back and know what was happening in the search.

'Anand's order has been clear. He will tell me once he gets any news about him' said the guard who came with us.

'Guys there is no use if we stay like this without eating' Avanti said.

'I'm not hungry' Kevin said. Malvika was about to say something, but didn't when Kevin gave her a stern look.

'If Rohit was here, he wouldn't have been sitting idly like this.' Avanti said. I could see pain in her eyes. It had swollen up and was blood red.

'Please' she murmured. Tears were trickling down her face. I got up and went to fetch some water. Priya joined me. Malvika went and hugged Avanti.

'Bro, we will find him' Geebi said and patted Kevin on his back. Kevin nodded.

#13

It wasn't a proper sleep. It was more like an exhaustion. She was etching something on the ground with a stone. Her eyes concentrating on the details of whatever she is doing. Her hair was fluttering in the slight breeze. I was wishing that this dream would never end.

It was then I realized that it wasn't a dream. Those beautiful pair of eyes was in front of me. Everyone else had dozed in front of the fire that was put up. Avanti was holding the walkie-talkie in one hand while writing something with the other. I couldn't help myself than to stare at her. She was remarkably cute but seemed exhausted.

'Hey' I said.

She smiled vaguely.

'Any information yet?'

She shook her head. I got her a cup of tea. My watch was ticking ten past two. It was pitch dark in all directions.

'Avanti get some rest' I said 'You are very tired.'

'No that is fine Sanjay. Besides I can't sleep now.'

'You should sleep. I will listen to the walkie-talkie.' She was keeping her hands over the fire. The winter was definitely coming.

'I will wake you up when I hear something. Now try sleeping Avanti' I insisted.

She was stubborn, 'No! Let's talk… Now I have you to talk'. She completed etching Rohit's name next to her.

'What do you want to talk?' I sat opposite to her.

Sipping her tea, 'Do you have any girl in your mind! I saw you looking at Parvati the other day' she winked.

'Oh she is a nice friend. That's it.' I said. Was she acting or she really doesn't know that I still had the remnants of crush for her. Girls can never be understood.

'Oh….' she took another sip of her tea. 'You do know your way around kitchen. This tea is good' she finished it.

I smiled. She smiled. There was this awkward silence. She didn't bother to break it. Rather she was decorating around the names she had written.

'So when are you planning to tell him?' I broke the bitter silence.

'I thought about telling him, when we came back from the peak. But then…'

I nodded.

'I will tell him the moment I see him the next time.' She said. 'But after punching him for leaving me and going.'

A smile was all I could put up. She started talking about how much she liked him and how much she missed him. I was just nodding to whatever she was saying. She moved and sat next to me. She gently placed her arm over mine and leaned on my shoulder.

'He will like me right?' she asked.

'Hmm...' I said. Why is she doing all this? Suddenly the walkie-talkie beeped.

'Mohan in 53.4. Come again.' It said.

'Anand here. Go ahead.'

'No sight of the boy. The site is secure.'

'Proceed till further command. Search for his clothes and shoes.'

'Heard loud and clear.'

Avanti got up and went to her tent. I couldn't stop her. I called the guard and informed what Anand had said. It reached our faculties' ear too. Everyone was awake because of the commotion.

'Madam how do you except us to go back without him?' Kevin asked.

Ms. Aydhika was quiet.

He continue, 'Madam he is just another of your students. But to us, he is our friend! He means a lot to all of us.' Kevin looked at all of us. Each and every word he said was from every one of our hearts.

'I agree Kevin' Ms. Aydhika said. 'But what about these students? Do they have to stay back too?'

'It's up to...' before Kevin could finish.

'I will stay back for my friend' Gopal said.

'Me too' said one of our classmate. And the whole camp echoed with the voice for Rohit. Ms. Aydhika was shocked. She desperately needed the support of Ramesh sir. And finally he came. His mere look made everyone silent. His eyes scanned the crowd and found Kevin. He was staring at him what seemed like an infinitely long time.

'He is right' he finally spoke. 'We cannot leave our student and go back home. The students roared like anything. Kevin shook his head and went near him. Ramesh sir was puzzled on Kevin's action.

'I am sorry sir; for what I did yesterday' he said.

'I forgot it the next instance. I envy your friendship' Ramesh sir smiled. He raised his arm to silence everyone. 'But on one condition!' The smile on Kevin's face suddenly disappeared. 'We can stay back only if these six people and rest of the students agree that we leave and no further delay.'

There was commotion everywhere. But he continued. 'I cannot further delay telling parents the real reason.' The depth of those words was high. If we didn't turn up on time, parents would be worried.

'What if we don't find Rohit before then?' I asked.

'Then we have to leave it to the forest guards to find him. Besides we don't know why he went.' He said bitterly.

Everyone was silent. No one dared to say yes and no one had the guts to say no.

'I take this silence as a Yes.' He said.

No cell phone range or network in the forest. So Ramesh sir and a forest guard went to city to inform the college authorities.

#14

As soon as the sun rose, we all walked back to the village and accommodated ourselves in the temple. It's work and craftsmanship was extraordinary. It had a very high compound wall. The deity was placed at the centre of the temple premises, beautifully surrounded by a pond on all four sides. The steps descending from this main temple gate had a wooden bridge that connected it to the inner sanctum.

The inner temple where the God's idol was kept and worshipped has been kept locked for months. Ramesh sir and Ranger Anand had requested the village chief to let us stay in the temple premises. We were to rest for the day in the temple Mandaps situated on either side of the bridge on the banks of the pond. Everyone felt comfortable and relaxed as it was a relief from the sunny morning; everyone, except us. We were finding ways to help the guards find Rohit.

'It will be a hard walk in the sunny day.' Anand said.

'We are ready to face it sir, we need to find him. That's all that matters.' I said. Anand said he would never agree on the girls coming for the search party. Malvika was the first one to say that she was fine staying back at the temple. It was difficult convincing Avanti. She was adamant on being part of everything that would help in finding him. It took a while for Priya to convince her. Priya understood the situation and went to find Veera. Geebi stayed back as he was completely exhausted. Kevin and I packed the necessary food and water and prepared to leave.

Avanti came running towards me. A thousand thoughts were running in my mind. But she said. 'Sanjay....' I was staring at her.

'Please bring him back....' she said. I nodded and went in search of him. Anand took us in a different route. The other guards were going down in different routes determined to not leave any path unexplored. Despite being a sunny day, we went ahead with all the energy we muster. Except water and berries, there wasn't anything to feed ourselves with. We went far and deep into the dense forest. The path had never seen any humans venturing through it.

'We are now in the heart of the forest' Anand said. He was holding a long stick to pave way for us. Kevin seemed fully energetic while I was struggling to go forward. The sun was punishing us with its continuous bolts of heat.

'I can't.... I will stay right here....' I said, 'You both go ahead. I wait here till you return.' Anand handed me a heat stroke tablet. I swallowed it without water as there wasn't any left. They went ahead. I stayed under an old Banyan tree to evade the heat of the sun. I thought of taking a small nap until they returned. My eyelids were drooping and the state of dream welcomed me…

She was holding him and he was playing with her hair. He lifted her chin. She closed her eyes as he bent and brought his face closer to her. He could feel her breathe over his face. Rohit went closer and closed the gap.

I jolted up from my sleep. It wasn't a dream I wanted to cherish so I forced to look around to fetch some water. All I knew was somewhere in the North there was a small reservoir. It wasn't easy to find the reservoir.

By the time I reached the reservoir, my thirst had disappeared. The mere sight of the reservoir was nauseating. The pure water of the reservoir was mixed with the frothing water from a small stream. I thought of following the stream to find where it was coming from. Just then I heard a vehicle's sound. A forest jeep was headed towards me. It stopped some hundred feet ahead of me. A person jumped out of it with a pistol in his hand. He pointed it towards me. I felt something poke causing a stringent pain inside me. I saw faces around me while my eyes finally closed.

Avantika

#15

I was really not in a mood to go and meet Veera. She is a beautiful and a nice girl, but she had suffered a lot for her age. I had to be positive that he would be back, my Rohit better be back. Priya had asked me to accompany her to Veera's house and I couldn't deny.

'Don't worry, he probably got lost. Sanjay and Kevin will find him' she said.

I absent mindedly nodded. Why does she have to mention Sanjay? It makes me feel miserable. I never wanted to hurt him. But at the same time I could not give him whatever he wanted. He had been my best buddy from school, still was a good friend. But that was it, there was nothing more than that. I didn't want him to be sad because of me. I tried my best to stay away from him. I knew that I was doing wrong lying on him. He thought I had slept even though I had not. At the moment, I didn't know what I was doing. It just felt right. Luckily the walkie-talkie beeped. Was I doing the right thing for him? For Rohit?

'It's locked!' said Priya.

'Maybe the neighbours would know' I said.

We went to the neighbouring house which had a small poultry for hen and cows in the shed built in front of their house. The sun was blazing hot. I took my dupatta and covered my head with it. Priya stood at the entrance and called to check if someone was in the house. An old man probably in his late seventies came out limping. His skin had fallen almost everywhere and his eyes were struggling to take in the brightness outside. Priya asked him about Veera. We noticed he had similar symptoms as that of Veera's mother. That made us wonder what was wrong in the village. People here were dying very often. Just then a small kid came out of the house. He was the same kid whom we had met at the temple. He recognised me immediately. I smiled at him. He hurriedly hid behind the old man's dhoti.

'Vasu what are you doing?' the old man asked pulling the kid in front.

'*Illa pa…*' Vasu said.

'So your name is Vasu' I said. He nodded and again went and hid behind the man's dhoti.

'Oh… you know my son from before?' the old man said pulling him again from behind.

'Your son…?' I asked. He more or less seemed like his grandson. Realising I was confused he said, 'I understand your confusion. I am just forty. It's because of this disease I look much older.' I didn't know how to respond to this. Priya understood I had stepped on a wrong foot. She quickly tried to revert the conversation back to Veera and asked 'Like I was asking, do you know where Veera is presently staying?'

'The village chief took her with him the very next day after her mother passed away' he said. 'Oh thank you uncle, you have been so helpful' Priya replied in Tamil. Geebi came hurtling towards us. He bent down and held his knee and was gasping for breath. Priya and I exchanged glances and I realised she was in the same state of shock.

'They have... they have brought back Sanjay. He is unconscious.' He said.

'What? Do you mean Rohit?' I asked hoping that he would say yes.

'No. Its Sanjay... he was unconscious when the forest guard Mohan found him. Kevin and Anand are back too.' He said. I felt the world falling around me. First Rohit, now Sanjay. We were running as quickly as we could to the temple.

'Is he alright? What happened??' I asked frantically unable to control my emotions. But Geebi wasn't responding. He was struggling to run as he was already drained out of stamina. When we reached the temple Mandap, we found it crowded with many villagers and our friends. My eyes were continuously searching for him, hoping that he would come out and stand by my side. More than Rohit I wanted to see him now.

In the middle of the Mandap, he was sitting with Kevin and holding his back. Anand was checking his eyelids. He was signalling them not to worry with his hand. And finally our eyes met. He smiled at me weakly with all the strength he could muster. To me that was more than anything I wanted at that moment. I ran and hugged him. It was a good feeling, but I didn't find him hugging me back. He must have been stupefied by my action.

'What happened?' I finally asked. The happiness that shone on his face was immeasurable.

He smilingly replied, 'Nothing Avanti…Its just dehydration. It was a hot day and we didn't carry much water with us.'

'But why did Mohan have to find you? Weren't you with Kevin and Anand?'

'Yes, I was. But the heat became unbearable so I decided to rest while they went ahead…' he took a break and looked at guard Mohan. 'He went in search of water and that drained him of completely.' Mohan completed.

'That's why I have been telling the authorities to close the forest during these months.' Anand said. Ramesh sir came forward and looked at Sanjay.

'This is it. We have stayed back and searched for him enough. Everyone here has suffered more than enjoying in the last few days. Also all the parents have been pressurizing the college for the actual reason of this delay. We cannot hide it anymore and cover it up with lame reasons.' He said turning towards us. 'I know everyone is really sorry for what has happened to Rohit, but he went on his own will,' he finished.

'But sir with all due respects, let not everyone stay here. Those who wish to stay can stay back and continue the search.' Kevin suggested.

'No Kevin! If something like what happened to Sanjay today happens to anyone else… Will you be there to save them always?' Sir thundered.

'And the forest is officially closed. I made a mistake by agreeing to your Principal.' Anand took a deep breath, 'I won't repeat it again.' He said.

'Yes, he is right...' I finally spoke.

'What the...' Geebi said

'Yes if Rohit has decided to go away without informing us, so let it be. We have waited enough for him to return. But he hasn't. It is his intention probably to be gone for long. Maybe he will come back by himself.' I said looking down. I knew everyone would be thinking badly about me. But then again I knew Rohit well enough, more than the rest of them would understand.

'How can you say something like that?' Kevin's anger was rising.

'If he was hurt or wounded, we would have already found him. But...' I said

'But?'

'But if he had decided not to come out, then we can never find him. Maybe we are just wasting our time.' Priya nodded. But Sanjay wasn't happy about this. I wanted to know what was going through his mind. I wished I was Edward Cullen from Twilight to read his mind. Once again he caught me staring at him.

'So that's it then. Pack your bags everyone!' Ramesh Sir said.

'Now that's not easy. We have to make a proper channel for you to go home.' Anand said.

#16

'Proper channel?' I asked. He nodded and started instructing the forest guards.

'Mohan get a statement from the people who stayed back on that day. File a copy in the office and a copy to collector office and media from the check post' Anand said.

Nothing was left for us to do. I helped Sanjay in getting up, but he neglected my help and leaped over Kevin and started walking. Geebi shook his head and walked back into the mandap. Malvika was watching all this.

'What did I do?' I asked.

'Nothing! You told them the truth.' She patted my back. 'Just give it some to sink in.' she said. We were informed that there would be a press meet in an hour and the collector would be addressing the issue.

I felt terrible because even Sanjay didn't understand me. Mohan came and collected the statement from Malvika and

Aydhika Ma'am. I went and sat on the steps on the bank of the pond. The cold water touching my feet made me shiver. Why did I act like that today? Was I doing wrong to Rohit, whom I liked the most? The more I thought about it, the more confused I became. Sanjay is just my friend, I kept on telling myself. I was looking at my reflection in the water. Another figure popped up behind me.

'Akka don't place your leg in the water. It's sacred for us' the voice said. I turned to see it was Veera.

'Oh sorry baby' I said as I lifted my leg. She pulled my cheeks and said, 'You look very cute Akka!'

'Thank you angel!' I said. 'Where are you staying now?'

'In the village chieftain's house with all the other children.'

'Oh... are there many more children like you in the village? How many are there?'

'Thirteen of us Akka' she said, 'and our Chieftain take care of us.'

Why didn't the people come out of the village for treatment? Even after thirteen children being orphaned, they hadn't even considered finding out the problem? I looked at the beautiful village in front of the temple, its lush green environment, its scenic beauty; it seemed like a paradise on Earth but cursed by this unknown disease. From the far end cars with siren were coming towards the village. It must be the Collector's vehicles. Veera was terrified as she was seeing so many vehicles for the first time. The parade of cars stopped in front of the brick building. We were asked to assemble there. Mohan came and took Malvika and Ms. Aydhika quickly to the brick building where the press meet was arranged. All the forest guards were running here and there to impress the collector.

'Akka bayama iruku' said Veera looking bewildered.

'Don't worry... It's just a formal meeting. I consoled her. I remembered having heard the Collector Dr. Chetan Sharma, IAS in one of the Ham radio meetings. At that time he was in Coimbatore. His formal dressing and prominent moustache made him an eminent person. He came out and went inside the brick building. Anand joined him inside. There were many television and newspaper reporters gathered around the brick building. Few had already started recording about the village and the college. Anand came out and asked Ms Aydhika and Malvika to come inside. Sanjay was staring at me. I intentionally never turned towards his side. I have done too many mistakes to feel sorry and regret about. Geebi was talking to Kevin and Priya. But when I went near them, they abruptly stopped whatever they were talking about. I think they were still angry at me. The Collector came out with Anand and the other two. He began addressing in Tamil.

'Today morning I received information about the boy who went missing a couple of days back. The witnesses have given me a statement that the boy named Rohit went to fetch some fruits inside the forest, but never returned after that. Since the forest is officially closed, all the other students are requested to vacate the reserved forest region immediately. I have arranged a special task force headed by ranger Anand.' Anand acknowledged. 'He and his team of forest guards will proceed as soon as possible and try finding him,' he finished and drank some water from the mineral water bottle.

The reporters began charging him with questions most of which he deflected and directed Anand to answer.

'Have the parents informed about the incident?' one of the reporters asked.

Ramesh pushed in and said, 'The college authorities are trying to contact his parents as we speak.'

'What do you think would have happened, ranger?' asked another.

'See let's not play any guessing game. It's about a boy's life. We can assure you that we will give our best in finding him.' Anand replied.

*   *   *   *

It was early next day morning. Chilling cold breeze was blowing in contradiction to previous day's climate. There wasn't anyone in the platform except us. The train was scheduled to arrive by five.

'Here drink this' Sanjay had brought me some tea.

I thanked him and took a sip. My body was shivering due to the fluctuations in the temperature.

'Avanti you are shuddering! Are you alright?' he checked my forehead for fever. He handed me his overcoat. 'Here, wear this, I will get you some medicines,' he said.

'No stay here. This is just the usual cold I get every morning.' I said and held his arm trying to pull him and make him stay. My mind was in a state of confusion unsure of my actions. But he freed his arm and went away nodding to join the rest of them. They seemed to be talking about something and Malvika didn't seem to agree with them. I kept my luggage down and went near them. Once again they suddenly stopped talking.

'Hey what's happening? What did I...? I burst out but stopped as the train hustled onto the platform with blaring horns and came to a halt.

'Let's get in. Geebi which compartment did you say we had our seats in?' Sanjay asked.

'D5. Right over there' Geebi answered. We got inside. No one seemed to bother about me. What had I done? I just said the truth. I thought not to argue with them. The train was unusually empty. I found myself a window seat and plugged in my ear pods. The train started moving and drifted beyond the station. The shuffle played a song in Sakthisree's voice and in A R Rahman's music from the album Kadal:

'Nenjukulle omma mudinjirukken
Inga yethisaiyil empozhappu vidinjirukko?'

Suddenly the train stopped. It was too early to come to the next station. In a half awake state, I looked outside the window. People got down from the train to check what had happened. But some of them were running into the dark. The person in the end turned back and saw me. It was Sanjay.

The train started moving again. What are they doing? Why did all five of them jump out of the train? Is that what they were planning? I went near the door, passengers were rushing in. I pushed them away and got near the door. Sanjay turned again and looked at the window where I was sitting. His eyes searched for me and finally fell at the door. I was dragging myself down the three steps of the train outside the door. My legs searched for the fourth step, but there wasn't any. The train was gaining speed. I took a leap of faith and let go of my hand. My left hand hit the ground and took the whole impact from the gravel stones. I rolled over to the sides. I could see Sanjay placing his hand over his head. The train has sped past me. My hand was bleeding and I felt dizzy. Before I closed my eyes, I saw him.

#17

It was a very beautiful place. For the first time I could see the fine line between the sea and the sky. As far as my eyes could see, it was just the sea shore. There was nothing but pearl white sand everywhere. The sky was totally blue without even a single cloud. For a moment I thought that the Sun wasn't there, but then it came abruptly appearing in the sky where I looked. The waves were playing a melancholy tune to my ears. 'Where was I? Why am I here?' I was searching answers to my questions, when I realized what had happened to me.

'Oh my God! Am I dead? Is this how heaven looks like?' My mind was wandering through the entire space. Then I saw him.

He was sitting on a boat. I missed him the most. His eyes, his face and the way he easily made me comfortable around him. He was smiling at me. The closer I got to him, the farther he went from me. He was getting out of my sight.

'Rohit…. Rohit…. Stay…. Don't go….' I cried.

'Priya! Malvika! She is opening her eyes.' shouted a familiar voice.

'Nurse….Nurse…. She is saying something.' came a voice from my left. I tried to open my eyes, but I couldn't even move a muscle. My hands were immovable as if nailed to the wall.

'Avanti….Avanti….Can you hear me?' Sanjay asked. Involuntarily I nodded. I opened my eyes as if I was in no hurry. Blurry images blurted out in front of me. It took me a few seconds to adjust to the brightness. My eyes were searching for that one person I wanted to see the most. The atmosphere was standstill in the room. The clock on the wall showed thirty past eight. Has it been morning already? How long have I been here?

'Please clear the room, let her breathe some fresh air.' Came a lady's voice. She flashed light in my eyes. It tingled. She finally switched it off.

'She is fine now. You can give her some food.' Nurse said. I tried to get up. Priya supported me and Malvika adjusted the bed so that I could sit. It was then I saw my hand. My left hand was completely covered with bandages. Through the glass door I saw Kevin. He was standing outside and talking to someone over phone.

'How long has it been?' I asked.

'It's the same day, evening. How are you feeling now?' Sanjay asked.

'Better.'

'Do you want anything to....' He was interrupted by the nurse.

'Please pay the remaining amount and for the medicines immediately.' She said and left.

Sanjay looked at me, 'As I was asking, do you want anything to eat?'

I wanted answers, not food. 'Leave all that.... Why did you all get down the train? Why didn't you tell me?' I looked at him. 'Why didn't you Sanjay?' He stayed silent. The smile on his face went out. I looked at Priya for answers. She became conscious of me looking at her.

'Avanti eat first. We will talk about it later.' She said. Kevin was still talking over the phone.

'No, I am not hungry now!' I was very stubborn.

'We didn't want to leave without Rohit. But you were okay with it.' I had never seen Priya getting angry like this before.

'I never said anything like that.... I wanted to find him, more than anyone.' I said. 'Seriously there has been a misunderstanding.' Priya nodded and looked at Kevin. She explained to me about the plan they had.

'Sanjay show her the map.' Priya said. Malvika gave me the hot idli that Geebi had brought. Sanjay opened a map. It was the same map that each group was given. Nothing seemed new in it. I looked at him hoping he would say something. He pointed somewhere on the map. It was a place called 'Adisuri'. I would have missed what he was trying to tell, if I hadn't looked closer. A small 'X' mark was marked near the place.

'What is this place?' I asked.

'We don't know anything about the place. But....' She paused.

'But?'

'We think that Rohit would have marked it.'

'Rohit?'

'Remember, he was the one who had the map all the time!'

'So you were planning to go there?'

She nodded.

'Even I want to come.' I said.

'No Avanti it's too risky' Geebi spoke. Kevin rushed in. 'We have to leave. Our parents know that we are in this hospital' Kevin beamed.

'How? Phone tracking?' Sanjay asked.

'No.... they haven't thought about it yet. He used Rohit's credit card to pay the bill.'

'Oh! There wasn't enough cash with any of us. And her bill was huge. I am sorry.' Geebi hung his face down.

'Forget it. Let's leave her here and go.' Kevin was quickly grabbing his stuffs from the room.

'I want to come!' I said and got up from the bed.

'No.... taking you will compromise our plan.' Kevin was making a rush and asked everyone to leave.

'I WANT TO COME! I LOVE HIM!' I shouted with all the strength left in me. Tears were trickling down my face. I couldn't lift my hand to hide the tears. Priya wiped my face.

'She is coming! Geebi get a taxi.' Priya said. Geebi and Sanjay left to get a cab. They took me through the back door of the hospital. Kevin was not happy with my presence. But none of this was running in my mind. Now I knew that Rohit was alive and he knew what he was doing.

#18

I was not comfortable in the Omni van. It felt like you were in an elongated car. And now that Sanjay was sitting next to me, it was making things more difficult. Malvika seem to be less bothered about what was going on. She had never put her IPod down. I even wondered if she worried about Rohit. Kevin was instructing the driver about the route from Google maps. Driver finally stopped the vehicle and said *'Enga poganumnu mattum sollu. Ippadi angayum ingayum sutha vekkatha.'* Kevin got irritated and showed the place on the phone, *'Inga poganum'*. The angry driver turned the vehicle and headed towards Ambasamuthiram.

'How are we planning to get inside the forest?' I asked.

'There is a small festival in the village tomorrow. So there will be preparations for it. So with little luck, we can get inside the forest, without the guards knowing.' Kevin said.

'Won't there be any guard at the check post?' I asked. 'How is it possible to leave the check post without anyone on duty?' I was thinking.

'Hmm….We are not giving an entry in the check post register and going.' Kevin said sarcastically. He looked at that driver, who was not bothered about whatever we are talking. Maybe he was happy that he got this long ride.

We reached Ambasamuthiram after an hour long journey. The Omni van stopped well ahead of the check post. Sanjay was staring at me the whole time. Was this his normal behaviour, or something else? Then I thought not to bother about it again.

'Five hundred is too much!' Sanjay said. 'The meter is showing only three fifty.'

'*Night charge thambi*' said the driver.

'*Adhellam mudiyathu na. Three fifty eduthukonga*' Sanjay said. The driver murmured and scolded us and left with what Sanjay gave. We began walking. The clock was ticking over five past ten. Geebi went to inspect the check post. 'As expected there was just one guard on duty and he too is sleeping.' he said. But we didn't take the risk. We skipped the check post and went directly into the forest. It was pitch dark and I was not able to see who was standing next to me. We couldn't risk the use of torch lights near the village as people might see us.

The village was right above us as we slithered through the forest under the cliff. We had been walking and walking for five hours to reach the base camp site near the Thenarru River. I thought of taking some rest before the sun rise as my hand was paining like hell.

'I can't take a step further' said Malvika.

'This is not the time to rest. If will be difficult to travel in the morning. We will be open to all wildlife.' Kevin said.

'And Kevin, holding my hand like this for long is causing me cramps' I said.

'This was the very reason why I said not to bring her.' He said. 'Because of her, everybody has to suffer.'

'Chill bro! If we don't rest now, we may not travel long tomorrow. Besides we don't have any food to eat' Sanjay said. The very mention of food created the reminder for hunger in my stomach. With my left hand hanging from the balance of my shoulder, it was difficult to walk straight for long. I desperately needed the rest. Kevin finally agreed as we were near the river.

This time we had to stay under the hundred million stars roof. The cool moon, the unusual silence and the freedom was an entirely a different feeling. Rohit come back to me. You are being dearly missed.

*   *   *   *

It was a barely a small nap. Kevin was pushing us to the limits. We were on our legs even before six in the morning. The place had extremes of climate. Nights were extremely cold and the days were awfully hot. The drowsy climate and the mild chill were making it difficult for us to walk. We did not bring our winter clothes. We never planned to stay for more than three days.

'Hey I remember this route. This is where I left Kevin and Anand so that I could get some rest' Sanjay said. 'I think I know the route. Show the map.' Geebi brought him the map.

'If we cross the hill, by walking along this tributary we could reach the smaller reservoir.' he paused. 'That's where I fainted.' he finished.

'Ok then. Let us go there. That will reduce the load of us carrying more water.' Malvika said. She was finally sparing some time away from the IPod.

'I doubt that! The water over there is undrinkable. It is full of froth and foam.'

'Let us minimize the use of water. If we reach there before noon, we can escape the heat of the Sun and even rest for some time.' Kevin said. Sanjay led the way. The beginning of Agasthya range had considerably low altitudes. We ventured through the small hills and reached the reservoir. As Sanjay said, the water was in really bad state. But nevertheless, we rested under the trees beside the reservoir. Kevin and Malvika went to fetch some fresh fruits. Priya went to investigate the reservoir for its frothy appearance. Geebi took out his Shepherd cap and covered his face. Sanjay was busily looking at the map. I tried to sleep, but my eyes weren't ready to close. I wandered here and there. Finally I steadied myself and sat next to him.

'What is it you are searching?' I asked.

'This 'X' mark. It is troubling me.' He said. I was looking at him for more answers. Besides, we did not know whether it was Rohit who had marked on the map. Looking at my confused state, 'Yes it is true we don't know whether Rohit did this or not!'

'Yes. Even if he did it, why would he go into the trouble of going to that place alone?' I asked. He could have told us, at least me.

'But what if he hadn't done it?' he asked. His eyes were still on the map.

'You mean to say someone would have inked it.'

'Could be. And he would have just gone to see what was so special about that place.' He said and looked at me. This seemed a possibility.

'Maybe....' I said. Suddenly there was a rustle of leaves from the dense foliage ahead of us. I looked at him. He was looking at the place from where the noise came. I searched for Priya; she was nowhere to be seen.

Geebi woke up. 'Are they back, those two?'

'Shhh....' Sanjay instructed. But he did not move his eyes. And then there was this heavy thud. A tree was pulled down.

'What is it Sanjay?' I couldn't see who was causing the noise. He slowly went behind me and woke Geebi. He whispered in my ears 'It's a lone tusker.'

'The lone what?' I asked. I was frightened before even knowing what it meant.

'It's an elephant. Single elephant.' Sanjay said.

'It is one only right?'

'If it comes as a herd, you don't have to worry. But if it comes out alone, then...' before he could finish, the elephant proved his point. It uprooted one more tree. Geebi was searching for something in his bag. The elephant had come out in open.

'Do not show any movement. Don't run.' Sanjay was hissing in our ears. The elephant was moving away to our left. Priya abruptly came from that side. I had Goosebumps all over me. She was happily walking in our direction. She realized the presence of the tusker, only when she saw us crouching in the corner. But it was too late. The elephant raised his trunk and made a thunderous trumpeting sound. Priya looked petrified and stuck at that place. From nowhere Geebi took a lit fire stick and ran in between the elephant and Priya. The fire and smoke from it chased the elephant away. It ran back into the forest.

Even when it had gone, the devastation it had done to the trees made me panic. Only when Sanjay went and checked the nearby area, I got up from the place. It was one of those moments when your heart tries to push out of the chest. It took me time to get over with my fear and panic. Malvika and Kevin came back after their hunt for food. Priya and Geebi explained about the incident. Malvika was listening with intense care, but Kevin was preoccupied with something in his mind.

With mangoes and few berries as our lunch, we continued down the reservoir and headed towards Adisuri, the place marked in the map.

#19

My hand had become better. Priya removed the bandages from my hand. Bruises covered my skin, reminding me of that incident.

The sky was getting dark. We had been walking along the reservoir for more than two hours. The pungent smell from the reservoir was nauseating for everyone. I closed my mouth with the dupatta.

'Is this the only way to go about Sanjay?' Malvika asked.

'This is the straight route to that place.' Sanjay said.

'Since it is getting dark, wouldn't it be better to stay on higher grounds?' Geebi asked.

'After what happened in the afternoon, I wouldn't mind straining myself to climb a hill' said Priya who was yet to come out of that trauma. Sanjay was checking the map for the closest and easiest spot to climb the hill.

'If we proceed further about a kilometre, there is this pine forest. It will be easy for us to climb.' Sanjay again led the way to the top of the hill.

It was an amazing view from top of the hill. The hill was bent in such a way that we could see the whole of Honey falls. Clouds were cascading over the hilltops. The fog was getting thicker and thicker. Each breath we let out immediately turned into a whitish vapour. It was only with the torch lights and mobile flash lights, we were able to see who was next to us. With utmost difficulty, we found a small moor on the top of the hill. It was the ideal spot for us to stay.

'We will rest here for the night. I will go find some firewood' said Sanjay.

'Wait…. I will come with you!' Geebi got a torch light and joined Sanjay.

'Meanwhile you people find some sticks to hold the tent.' Sanjay said and left. It was pitch dark except for a number of torch lights. I tied together whatever shawls and dupatta Priya and I had and made into a one single large cloth. Malvika prefers jeans and Tee to salwar and kurtas. So there was not any contribution from her for the tent canvas. But on the other hand, Kevin had a few scarfs. I was wondering how the trends had changed in men and women's clothing.

'Does Sanjay have any of these?' I asked.

'Check his bag. He may have one or two.' Kevin replied. He was busy doing some heavy duty stuffs like carrying heavy rocks and pitching the tent. He seemed to be fit and muscular. Maybe that is why Malvika fell for him. My thoughts went to Rohit. He was the fittest person I had ever seen. I got to see his upper body with packs once when we all went to Kovai Kuttralam. I could still picture those images in my mind. We will find you soon Rohit, I thought.

The tent was finally raised. But those two were not back yet. It was getting colder every minute. The mercury hung low in the thermometer. I was getting scared. My mind was imagining deadliest of things. What if the elephant came back? What if they were bitten by some venomous snakes? What if they slipped and fell off a cliff? Oh God! Why am I imagining such things. Our mind is very tricky. When you tell it not to do something, it will devote itself as a whole to it. But to put a dot over my imaginations, they came back.

Sanjay and Geebi dropped all the wood outside the tent and came inside. From his look, we could make out something was wrong. He was breathing heavily. I offered him a place to sit. Since we had less number of clothes, the place was very cramped. If I slept at one corner, my legs would have hit the face of another person. He sat down and Geebi beside him.

'What happened?' finally Kevin broke the silence.

'We saw lights in the valley of Adisuri.' Sanjay said. 'I think people are down there.'

'It could be Anand and forest guards searching for Rohit.' Priya said.

'No the lights were coming from over a large area. And the lights were not moving.' Geebi said.

'Let us not bother about it now. We will check it out in the morning as the first thing' Kevin said.

'And I will stay guard outside, just in case.' Sanjay said.

'No I will stay bro! You get some rest!' Kevin pushed us all and came out of the tent. Only when all the other people came out, the innermost person in the tent could come out. But Kevin rushed outside, pushing the tent to slide on one side.

'Kevin! Go repair the tent first.' Priya said. She was the one who had calculated the measurements for the tent.

'We will take turns. I will wake you up after an hour or two. But repair the tent first.' Sanjay said. He went outside to stand sentinel for the night. I missed my Ham! I had even planned to broadcast about my trip this week. But in the present situation, I didn't think it was possible. I hoped my regular tuners; the old couple from Bengaluru didn't get disappointed. I dosed off into the dream world.

It was again the same horrible dream I was getting the past few days. I was leaving behind something and was running. Someone was running along with me. Whatever I left behind was something very important to me. But how much ever I tried, I could not get to know what it was or who was running with me.

Sanjay was still outside staying guard for us. He was shivering. He was just wearing a thin shirt. I got up and gave back his pull over. He smiled and took it from me.

'What time is it?' I asked.

'Thirty past two.' He said.

'Oh then why are you still here? Didn't Kevin get up?'

'I tried waking him up, but he didn't move a muscle. Poor fellow, let him rest for some time.'

'Ok then, I will stand guard. You sleep now. It will be dawn soon.'

'No, it is fine.'

'Sanjay you are shivering. Get some rest. Anyway, I was not getting any sleep. So I will stay up for some time.'

I said. I wished that he would say that he would stay back to talk with me.

'Are you sure?'

'Yes I am! You desperately need some rest.' I smiled. 'Sanjay, say you want to talk to me. Don't sleep now.' I was whispering to myself.

'Okay then good night!'

'Good night.' He did not even wait for my reply. I really have to control my mind. I needed to stop feeling guilty about him. But the other half of my mind was happy when he was around.

#20

It was the same dream again. I was holding someone's hand and running away from it. But this time too I couldn't find what it was. Was it some animal like the elephant? Was I scared when I was running? I could barely remember it now. I wondered if Rohit was having the same dream. I should ask him when I meet him. It was better to stay awake rather than have this dream again. I looked inside the tent, everyone was happily sleeping. Malvika's leg was over Geebi's hair and his leg was near Sanjay's face. Good that I decided to stay awake.

The sky was perfectly clear. The pure air here made sure that the diamonds of the sky were properly visible. The waxing moon was sending her radiance down upon us. Full moon was not far away. Who could be it? Those lights that Sanjay and Geebi saw. I looked again inside the tent. Everyone was yet to come out of their sleep. 'They wouldn't mind. I will be back before they wake up.' I said to myself. I took one of the torches from Sanjay's bag and came out the tent. 'Don't I need the map?' I asked myself. Again I went inside and took out the map from his bag. While coming out I accidently stamped Geebi's leg, but he was snoring in his deepest sleep. I had a sigh of relief when I finally came out of the tent without waking anyone.

I beamed the torch light to see on which way to go. Sanjay had already pointed out our current location on the map. The cliff was just about ten minutes' walk from this place. From there I could clearly see the valley of Adisuri. I closed the map and tucked it inside my backpack and headed for the cliff. The path was filled with rattling and hissing noises. How stupid of me to come out at this hour to the unknown forest alone! Only the torch light guided the way for me. But very soon the fear was gone. I reached near the very edge of the mountain.

He was right. This light was not for the few forest guards. The entire valley was glowing with white lights. I could not believe my own eyes. It was like an entire city hidden behind the forests. What could be happening in this place? Does Anand know about this? My mind was racing for answers. I sat down by a rock to see if anything happened. Suddenly the fog thickened, masking my view. I could see only the obscure images of the valley. The fog brought the freezing cold with it and I didn't have any shawl or dupatta to cover myself. I hated my bad luck.

Then it struck me. This must be the stone quarry that Veera's mother and other villagers were working in. I looked at my watch, 'I should get back now' I said to myself. Luckily no one was awake by then.

'Were you awake the whole night?' Sanjay asked the first thing in the morning. I nodded. 'Should I ask him about the dream?' My mind was yet to come to a decision.

'Is everything fine?' he asked looking at my confused face. I nodded again.

'Are you thinking on how your parents will be reacting to this' he came up with a fair guess. Only after his mentioning did I really think about them. All our parents would have complained about the administration of the college. This would have gone to media. Our names and photos will be flashing across all local news channels.

'What would your parents be thinking?' I asked him.

'I guess they will try to understand the situation.' He said. I gave him a blank look.

'You see, we all wrote a letter to our parents saying that we will return in a couple of days and asked them not to worry. But since you were' he paused, 'since we didn't know what was on your mind, we didn't send a letter to your parents.'

'Oh hmm....' They had planned it very carefully, I thought. So only Rohit's and my parents will be searching for us. I was lost in my own thought processing world. Sanjay got up and started walking away.

'Sanjay... ' I called. He turned back and questioned me with his hands.

'How was your sleep?' I didn't know how to ask him about it.

'Oh I had a sound sleep. I was in much need of that rest.' He replied.

'Oh did you have good dreams?'

'Hmm… I don't remember my dreams and they are vague.' He said and walked away. So it was only me then. We had the same fruits and berries to fill our stomach and headed for the valley of Adisuri. The Sun was high and shining. We could see the valley very clearly.

'It doesn't seem like the rock quarry' Geebi said. It really didn't. There were four huge buildings aligned side by side in the shape of 'L'. Enclosed by it was long length roof tiled structures which had three openings that ran to our hill. It could be some tunnel.

'Should we go ahead?' Priya asked.

'It looks very creepy! I don't want to take the risk!' Malvika backed out.

'What if Rohit is there? Will you do the same thing still?' Kevin was again in his peak anger form. Malvika remained silent.

'I think it is better that we take a closer look' Sanjay suggested. We decided to drop to a low altitude and know what exactly was happening out here. We were following Sanjay's footsteps. It was the steep side of the mountain. Descending down was more or less like hanging by a wall. We had to be careful on placing our steps; one small misplacement, we would fall the whole 2000 feet down. I was carefully watching my steps, but something caught my attention. It was hanging by its lace on both the sides of a branch. If it was not for the bright colour and its brand, I wouldn't have noticed that shoe. It was a Nike bright blue Sports shoe, the same shoe that I gave Rohit for his twentieth birthday. I stopped to grab the hanging shoe.

'Priya…. Sanjay… Geebi stop!' I cried holding on to that branch. Kevin and Sanjay were in the front and Malvika was just behind them. Geebi was helping Priya to cross a thorny bush. Everyone panicked and turned back to see what had happened. I held the shoes in one hand while holding to the tree on the other hand and cried 'Rohit's shoes.'

I could see the shock on their face. They could not come back as the path was too narrow. My mind was not responding. It was failing to accept the falling pieces into the picture and kept on searching for that one missing miracle piece. He was around here was the only pleasant thought that was running in my mind. Whatever this place was, it had a strong connection to Rohit. It is what people call as gut feeling. You believe even when the odds are not in your favour.

Sanjay helped me in getting down a huge rock. Trees were covering most of the place but we could clearly see people of around Veera's mother's age carrying something over their head in baskets. They were coming out of those lanes that were leading to the underside of the hill.

He asked for the shoes. I showed him.

'Are you sure this is his?' Sanjay asked.

I nodded. 'I bought him these shoes. It's the same size nine.' I said. The look on his face suddenly changed.

'He must be here somewhere close by. Let us go down and inquire about him to those people.' Kevin said.

'I don't think it is good idea to go down there together.' Sanjay said. 'Let me and Kevin go and enquire about Rohit.' I was watching them till they were crowned by the trees of Adisuri. Malvika was observing something on the ground.

'What is it?' I asked. She did not have to explain. The very florescent colour explained. But it was not a butterfly or flower or a living thing for that matter, it was a stone.

'I don't know. It could be some rare mineral.' she said and safe guarded in her bag. I sat by a rock and looked at his shoes. What was Rohit doing here? Was he is some trouble or was he here to satisfy his urge to know more.

Geebi was looking at the shoes too. He came and sat next to me. 'You really miss him…. Don't you?' he asked.

I nodded and smiled. 'Geebi can I ask you something?'

'Go ahead.'

'Have you ever got a dream that keeps on repeating, day after day?'

'I rarely get dreams other than Kareena and Priyanka!' he blushed. 'Why, do you get the same dream regularly?' he asked.

'Yes!'

'What is it in the dream that makes you so worried?'

'It could be nothing. But I could never complete the dream.'

'Enlighten me with me your dream Avanti! I will try to help you out.' he said. He was a person who would give a truthful opinion. If I needed a decision to make or a person to pour out my fears, Geebi was the first person I would think of. His cut and right approach to any problem and the wise decisions he made, made him the Aerospace department representative. I explained him my dream, each and every part of it. It was registered deep in my mind now. He was staying calm for a long time now.

'Where do you think this dream was happening?' he finally asked.

'I am not sure. It was like a house.' I said 'No no…. it was more like a forest.' I was confused now.

'Whom do you think it was holding your hands?'

'I couldn't see the face Geebi.'

'Try harder…' he said.

'I don't know who it was.' I said. 'I wish its Rohit.' I said to myself.

'Was it day or night in the dream?'

'I don't remember.' I never thought about it. And now when he asked, I couldn't recollect it.

'Do you remember….' before Geebi could finish, there was this swift striking sound from the valley. I looked at Priya. She too was in a confused state. And then one more sound and this time I could make out what sound it was. It was the firing of the gun.

'It's the gun…' Geebi panicked. Sanjay and Kevin were down there. What would have happened to them? I couldn't think straight.

'I will go check….' Geebi said.

'No…. Stay here. Take care of them. I will find out what has happened.' I said. Malvika was dead scared. 'This is why I asked them not to go down.' She said and started crying.

'Shhh…. Don't worry! I will go check and come back with them.' I said and left. What if the unthinkable happens? Will they come and search for them too? I went back and said, 'If I don't come back within half an hour, return to the village and inform the ranger Anand.'

'But….' Priya began.

'No ifs and buts. Leave, if we don't come back'. I felt that I was safeguarding them.

I climbed down the rest of the hill. More and more thorny bushes were covering the ground. At a distance I could see one of the lanes that were coming from the hill's bottom side. I looked around and there wasn't anybody around. I proceeded to the lane. It was very dusty around the lane and I was walking on it. On the sides there were these small luminescent stones, similar to what Malvika had found. What was going on here? I asked myself. Suddenly I felt a hand on my shoulder. I shrieked and pushed that hand away. Before I could react, one more hand covered my mouth. I bit the hand that was covering my mouth and pushed harder till I saw that hand. The band in his hand was a Lord Shiva band. And I knew only one person who had that band. I stopped fighting back.

'You idiot! It hurts' Sanjay whispered.

'I am sorry.' I said. Kevin kept on looking around. 'What happened? That sound!' I asked.

'Will tell you…. It is not safe here. Let us first get out of here.' Sanjay said. 'You came here all alone?' he asked.

I nodded. Then suddenly, I heard the same bullet sound again, but this time closer. The bullet passed between me and Kevin and hit the tree behind me. I tried to see who it was. But Sanjay pushed my head down and gestured to run. Bullets were randomly passing between us. I ran with all I could. Thorns were slicing through my skin. Sanjay was running next to me and Kevin little ahead of us. I couldn't run anymore. My knees were pulling me down. We were fairly away from them.

'Sanjay…. Sanjay….' I called him.

'Little more Avanti. We will reach the reservoir.'

'I can't….' I said and stopped. Blood was soaking my pant red. He pulled me behind a tree and called Kevin to stop going further. He pulled my leg to find the source of the blood.

'Ahhh….that hurts' I screamed in pain.

'Shhh….' He closed my mouth with his hand. The pain was excruciating. First my hand and now it's my leg. Somewhere in my lower left thigh, there was a thorn that had penetrated into my skin. Sanjay carefully pulled it out. My blood was oozing out from where an inch long thorn was a minute back. He tore my dupatta and tied it around the wound.

'Hold it tight till it stops.' He said and went about to check if the way was easy for me to go. I tried to get up and walk. Kevin helped me to get up.

'What is happening here? Who was it, chasing us?' I asked. I was limping and hanging by his shoulders.

'I don't think you can climb up the hill.' Sanjay decided.

'Oh is there a way back to village, without the climbing part?' I asked.

Sanjay checked the map, 'We could go, but what about Geebi and others? How will they come?'

'Oh they will come back directly to village! I have instructed them' I said. Sanjay was satisfied on how I had handled the matter. 'Now tell me who was it, chasing us?'

'Forest guard Mohan.' Kevin replied.

#21

'What the....' I was in a state beyond the shock. Why was he shooting us? He was with us all the time. I composed my mind, 'Why was he shooting us?'

'Show her.' Sanjay said.

'But...' Kevin hesitated.

'Show me what? Why hesitation Kevin, show me whatever it is!' I said. My heart was pumping more blood than normal. Kevin took out his mobile and gave it to me with reluctance. It was having a video on its screen. I clicked it play.

What I saw drained the life out of me. It was an open area, where two people were standing. The more closely I looked; I could see their hands and legs tied together. They looked scared. They both kept on looking at each other. Then, he came with a gun in his hand. The two people went on their knees and looked around for help. When they turned, I could see the cloth that was tied around their mouths. The man fell at Mohan's feet. Mohan didn't bother looking down. He loaded his gun and shot the lady. She fell silent on the ground. The man just then realized that the lady was dead. He was crying over the lifeless body of the lady. Mohan took out a camera from the man's bag and thrashed it on the ground. Then one more shot. The man fell over the lady, dead.

I dropped the mobile. 'What kind of world am I living in?' was the first thought that was running in my mind. I have seen such things in movies, but seeing a cold blooded murder was like sucking the life out of you. Kevin picked up the phone.

'How did you happen to capture this? ' I asked.

'We were roaming around in search of anyone to talk. But then we saw these building and the lanes. No one was there in the building. So we came outside and that's when we saw this.' Kevin said. When they were walking they heard Mohan speak. Mohan was saying something like not to leave anyone from the family in the walkie-talkie. Then he came out in the middle and shot those two people.

'But why was he chasing us?' I asked.

'He got a call from his walkie talkie. Suddenly he went back inside the building and came out with one more gun for his left hand.' Sanjay said. 'We thought of leaving immediately. But that is when you came.'

'From the moment you came down, he was tracking you. He got a call again in his walkie talkie. We used this time to get to you and escape. But he saw us.' Kevin explained. I couldn't even imagine what would have happened to Rohit. 'He is alive…. He is alive!' I was saying it to myself.

'It is better not to stay here for long! Let us go and meet our friends in the village.' suggested Sanjay.

After a long four hours of hiking, we reached the village. It was a very different scene now in the village. The roads were richly decorated with flowers and there were lamps in front of every house. My eyes were searching for Geebi, Priya and Malvika. They were nowhere to be seen. People were looking alien to our presence. We didn't bother much and went ahead to the brick building to meet Anand. If there was one person, who could help us now, it would be him.

'Is it safe to trust him?' Kevin asked.

'He is the best chance we have.' I said. He was with us all the time. And I was sure he would take action against Mohan.

We saw him come out of the brick building. He was about to get into the jeep.

'Sir!' we called out to him in unison.

'Oh! You!' he got down from the jeep. We looked at him to say something. But all he did was smile.

'You have caused a lot of trouble! And guess what, you have made the headlines of almost all the newspapers and TV reporters.' he said.

'Sir…. We are sorry. But….' Sanjay said.

'Did you find your friend?' he asked.

We shook our head.

'Never mind! Atleast you all came back!' he paused. 'What about the others? I heard that all six of you did the stunt of jumping out of the train!'

It was nice when someone mentions that we did some stunts. 'Wait, aren't the others back yet?' I asked. I could sense Kevin and Sanjay staring at me with questions on their face.

'No they haven't!' Anand said. Now what had happened? Had Mohan caught them? It would all be because of me again.

'Is there a problem?' Anand asked.

'Sir…. Its Forest guard Mohan.' Sanjay hesitated.

'Yes what about him?' Anand was puzzled at the expression on Sanjay's face.

'Sir he has killed two people!' Kevin said and took out his phone. Anand was shaken by what he saw in the phone.

'Sir also there is something happening inside the forest and it doesn't look normal.' Kevin said.

'And I guess he would have caught our friends too now.' I said. I have been making a lot of mistakes. But this one had caused irreparable damages. My friends had been caught because of my foolishness.

'This is outrageous. Let me file a complaint with the Collectorate office.' Anand said.

'No sir…. Not yet! If what Avanti said was true, then we should go get our friends back.' Sanjay said. He thought for a while and went back inside the brick building and came back with a gun.

'You people stay here, I will go find out what is happening out there!' Anand said.

'Sir we will come too!' Kevin said.

'No, enough of the troubles you have caused! Let me handle this.' he said.

'Sir what if there were many people with Mohan?' Kevin asked. Anand was thinking on what Kevin had said.

'Fine, on one condition. You should agree on whatever I say.' Anand said. We all nodded.

*   *   *   *

We reached the place where Mohan shot the man and the lady. It was pitch dark except for the bright light in the centre of the four buildings. It was like a stadium with poorly lit lights.

'Wait here till I find him.' Anand said and went into the dark. I could hear some machine running in the close by buildings. Then suddenly there was some movement in the centre. Three people with their hands tied were walking to the centre of the lighted zone. They kept on looking back, but there was no one to be found. Their faces were familiar. Priya was badly injured. I could see the blood stains over her dress near her elbow. Malvika was crying the whole time she was walking. Geebi was not showing any emotion on his face.

'Kevin stop!' before Sanjay said, Kevin was running towards them. Malvika was crying even more loudly. 'It's a trap Kevin! Go back!' she was shouting.

I looked at Sanjay. He was looking somewhere behind me. I turned back and saw him. He was holding the gun, pointed towards us. Mohan made us walk silently towards the rest of us. Kevin was hurriedly untying the knots from Malvika's hand. Mohan shot a bullet in the night sky to show his presence.

I then knew that it was over. We were all going to die here, like the man and the lady. It was my mistake that six of my friends are going to breathe their last breath down here. He made me and Sanjay stand near them. I could see fear in everyone's eyes. Then I remembered, Anand. He would come up with some plan to rescue us. It was a small ray of hope that bloomed inside me.

Finally he spoke. 'I never wanted to do this! But you leave me with no choice.' Mohan pointed the gun at Sanjay's head.

'Stop it Mohan!' a voice thrashed into the doom of silence. Anand was pointing the gun on Mohan. There was this silence that concealed this place. Mohan lowered his gun. Anand lowered his too. If I was not wrong, I saw Anand smiling. He walked towards him. We were confused by the change in Anand's behaviour.

'Immature kids, they trusted the wrong person!' Anand said.

#22

I could not get the grip of the situation. Or I was finding it difficult to believe what I was seeing. This was not like the Ranger Anand we knew. Anand gave the plaster to Malvika and made her tie it around our hands. She did as she was asked! Anand made her sit next to me and tied her hands too.

'No need for all of this. Let's finish them here!' Mohan said and raised his gun again. 'They have given us lot of trouble.' My heart was pounding in my chest.

'No, it is not that simple. We have to find him.' Anand said. 'And to get him, these are our baits.' Mohan lowered his weapon. Who was he talking about? Is it Rohit? Is Rohit out there all alone? My mind was wandering in my own thoughts.

'Oh yes, your friend Rohit knew about us.' Anand said. 'But he escaped!'

'Not for long!' Mohan said and laughed. Anand and Mohan were discussing something.

Everyone was silent. 'What are they doing here? Why did they tie us?' I asked.

'They are doing some sort of illegal mining! That is what we heard when we were tied down inside that room.' Geebi said.

'What is happening here? Why have you tied us?' Kevin shouted. Mohan raised his gun again. Anand silenced him.

'What do you know Kevin?' Anand asked him.

'I know that he killed two people!' Kevin was staring at Mohan. 'But there is something more than that isn't it?'

'Yes! We have been doing international business from this forest! This same old forest' he said.

'Anand…. What are you doing?' Mohan tried to stop Anand from telling more.

'Shhh….' He silenced Mohan.

'Yes Kevin, he killed those two people. Because they tried to expose our world out to the public. But you people are even more foolish. Came directly to me, complaining about him.' He started laughing. 'Fools, I gave him the order to kill those two reporters.' Mohan joined him in the sinful and proud laughter.

'How can you laugh when you have killed two people? Are you not ashamed?' Priya asked.

'Ashamed! Why should we be ashamed?' Mohan answered. 'Sneaking into other's life, publicizing their personal life and destroying them. This is what reporters do! I don't feel ashamed of killing such people.'

'You are destroying Government's forest. That is not your personal life!' I said.

'Government's forest!' Anand looked around. 'From the fruits you eat to the clothes you wear, everything comes from forests like this. What has the Government done to us apart from recognizing us as a vote bank.' he looked straight at my eyes. 'For each and every day of their life, they need resources from us! But when we asked for the basic amenities, where was the Government?' Anand said.

We stayed quiet. 'So the next time you speak, think and speak!' he said. 'Mohan tie them in the machinery room. We need them to catch their friend.' Anand started walking away from us. 'And don't leave them near any instruments or scrap materials. These are engineering minds, they think.' he left.

Mohan tied us in one of the rooms. It had piles and piles of rocks. It was nothing but rocks everywhere. He brought us away from the piles and tied us around a pole using steel chains. He locked the room from outside.

'That's it. We are stuck here. And when they catch Rohit, we all will be dead.' Malvika was weeping.

'Stop it! We will find a way and it's only two of them.' Kevin consoled her. He tried to break himself loose, but couldn't. But what caught my attention were the yellowish rocks in the huge pile. They tended to emit some light and glitter. Sanjay was noticing the same stones. He extended his leg and reached a stone among the ones that were scattered over the ground. He moved it around and brought it near him. The stone was made of numerous layers of yellow and grey soil.

'What could be this?' Sanjay pushed the stone towards me with the legs.

'I don't know. It could be some rare mineral.' I said. Sanjay nodded. There was nothing much we could do. Kevin had been scratching the metal chain on the ground in a desperate attempt to break it. But it was very strong and heavy.

'Guys what do you think Rohit is up to?' Geebi asked. He was sitting right behind me over the pole.

'He would have known about this place right.' I asked. I strangely felt his presence here.

'He would have! His shoes were found here.' Sanjay explained. Someone was trying to open the door. The click on the lock and the sound of levers turning as the key was inserted was clearly heard. Mohan came and asked us to drop our mobile phones and our other belongings. He took out even our watches. Then he locked us back inside.

My hands were getting numb. It was let free only when we were to eat. It has been two days since we came into this room. We were becoming claustrophobic, whenever Anand or Mohan opened the door. Every time they came in, we wished that it was only for the food and not to end our lives. Everyone feared that when Rohit was caught, we would die. The very reason for which we had come back had now turned against us. Kevin never stopped working on making the chain break, even though he knew it was highly impossible. Was Rohit aware of all this? Does he know that his friends came back for him? My mind was boiling with so many thoughts, but none seemed to give me the answer I wanted.

Mohan had just given us food and went outside. Suddenly another man entered the room with a shovel in his hand. I recognized him at once. He was that old neighbour of Veera. I could see he was confused on seeing us.

'Sir help us! He has captured us and has locked us down here.' Priya was pleading. Before he could react, Mohan came inside the room.

'What are you doing here?' he shouted.

'Sir, you asked to clear the pile from this warehouse.' he replied.

'That's not this one, its next one.' Mohan said and pulled the man outside the room.

'Sir, Anand was saying that those students were missing....' Before he could finish, Mohan closed the door again.

#23

It's the fourth day of staying in this room. There wasn't any light except the small hole on the asbestos sheet. A small feeling was getting developed inside me. I was feeling that Anand's argument was correct. It was turning into empathy towards him. I even argued with my friends, when they were discussing on how crooked Anand had been acting in front of us.

'What's wrong with you?' frustrated Kevin asked on my sudden change in behaviour.

'No, I am just saying that what they are doing is also right!' I defended myself.

'Oh! According to you, he holding us as bait is not wrong at all, is it?' Kevin was scratching the metal chain even more vigorously over the ground.

'No, this is wrong. But if we hadn't come back, then we would not have seen this side of Anand.' I said. It made sense to me. I didn't know why others weren't finding it that way.

'Stop it…. Don't say another word.' irritated Kevin said. Snap! The sound created goosebumps inside me. The metal chain that Kevin was scratching has snapped open. Since it was a single chain that was wrapped around everyone, his job became much easier.

We got up from the place; it was a wonderful feeling after we got ourselves free. It felt like we had got the keys of our life back. But it was Kevin's hard work and determination that paved the way.

'Let us get out of here, before he or Anand comes back again.' Malvika was smiling after all these days.

'Not so easy. Even though it is night now, this is their land. We have to be careful' Kevin said. He went near the door and peeped through the keyhole. 'He is coming.' He said and ran back to the pole. We sat as we were sitting, and placed the chains as it was before. Mohan unlocked the door and came inside. Immediately he could sense that something had happened. He took out his gun and checked every corner of the warehouse.

'Did he come here?' he asked.

We stayed quiet. 'Answer now, is he here, Rohit?' he asked.

'What Rohit? Is he here?' I asked.

'Don't act…. If I find out, you all will be dead!' he said and went out. We didn't do anything. Then he came back in and straight to us. He unlocked us from the pole. We were holding the chain as it was trying to fall. We managed to hide it from Mohan.

'Hmmm come outside.' Mohan pushed us outside. We did not say anything and kept walking. The centre opening was lighted like I saw in the video. He made us stand in the centre. Anand was loading his gun with bullets. He came towards us. He pointed the gun to my forehead.

'Rohit I know you are around here somewhere. Enough of playing hide and seek. I am going to count till three. If you don't turn up, I will kill this girl and go for one more round.' He said. My heart was pounding faster. I hoped he didn't turn up. I didn't mind dying for him.

'One....' he shouted. I closed my eyes. I could see my parents face, all those happy moments I shared with them. Then came my friends who have been there for me always. Then his face appeared. I had had a happy life with the people I loved and I was content.

'Two....' I could feel his force of the gun against my temple. The barrel was pressing me harder in the head. Then it happened all of a sudden. It was fully dark like all the lights have been sucked out of your life. No one was to be seen. But there was this pressure still in my head. Anand didn't take his gun out of my head. I opened my eyes. It was dark outside; even the dimly lit lights were gone.

'Mohan what happened?' Anand shouted. There was no response. 'Mohan!' he shouted again. No sound came from the side where Mohan was standing.

There was a faint light that was coming towards us. Anand was holding my hand tightly. It was coming faster and faster. Not until it came very close, I would have guessed who it was. It was him. It was for him, that we came back. It was Rohit. But Anand didn't see that coming. Rohit placed a heavy fist punch over Anand's face. The hand that was holding me fell down. Rohit picked up the gun.

'Do you have the keys for the chain?' he asked.

'No need of that, we are free' Kevin said.

'Excellent' Rohit breathed. 'Let's get out of here before Mohan comes.' He held my hand and adjusted the head lamp with the other hand. We didn't wait even for a second and sprinted out of that place.

'Anand sir! Anand sir!' we could hear Mohan searching for Anand in the dark. Then he saw the light from Rohit's head.

'Rohit!' he shouted and was coming towards us.

'Rohit... lights.' I warned him. He immediately switched it off.

'Over here.' he said and turned towards the hill side. 'He has torch lights. We can't beat him in this forest. We will hide over by the trees.' We followed him wherever he was leading us. Rohit made us hide behind a huge trunk of a tree. From a long distance, we could see another white light headed our way.

'Shhh... stay silent' whispered Rohit. Nothing else was heard except our breathing. Rohit's hand was still holding mine. I was on cloud nine. Even stuck in this situation, I was happier than ever. It was feeling beyond words. Mohan was closing in on us. He flashed the torch lights all around while walking. We had camouflaged ourselves with the creepers. Rohit gripped my hand tightly. Mohan came near us flashed the light above us. We had bent ourselves and sat on the ground to the knee level. We sat like a statues, not moving even a muscle. Finally Mohan gave up and went ahead to search. Rohit loosened his grip and removed his hand. I wish he had kept like that for some more time.

'It is still not safe. He will come back.' Sanjay said.

'Let's go forward to Vettumalai. We can stay over there for the night.' Rohit said. We walked as he guided us. I was admiring him the whole time. But no one else spoke a word. The fear that we had just missed our death and it may come back soon to catch us made us very cautious.

Vettumalai was a place near the Honey falls. It was densely covered with trees and shrubs. 'Even during the day, it would be impossible to find us here' Rohit said. 'And also I have a secret place near the hill, it would be impossible for them to come up there.' He seems to know the way around here. He took turn at a particular point and went forward.

'Be careful, the rocks are slippery.' He said and lend me his hand again. I couldn't see his face with that torch light that he used to show over the rocks. With little effort and proper guiding, we reached that special place that Rohit had mentioned. It was not a cave, but a small opening in the middle of the hill. There were fruits and a mat made of coconut leaves inside the cave.

Kevin didn't wait any further. 'How dare you! How dare you leave us and go.' Kevin said and pushed him over the wall. Rohit didn't resist. That small fight ended very soon. Kevin hugged him and Sanjay joined them. When he was let free by both of them, Geebi jumped at him. 'Missed you bro!'

'Me too!' Rohit replied. Priya was in tears. 'We were really scared for you.' She said and hugged him. 'Never do this again' Malvika said. He nodded and smiled.

I didn't say anything and stood there quietly. He came towards me. 'Are you still angry at me?' I didn't say anything and went outside the cave. He followed me.

'I am sorry' he said. I turned my head. 'I am sorry. I am sorry. I am sorry' he pleaded. I still didn't turn. He deserved it. He made me wait for this long. Let him wait for some more time. But he had other plans. He pulled me from back and hugged me and whispered 'I am really sorry.' I couldn't resist anymore. I turned back and hugged him tightly.

'Don't ever leave me anymore.' I whispered in his ears.

'I won't.' he said.

'I missed you Rohit.'

'You don't have to anymore.' He said and lifted my face. He looked straight into my eyes. I couldn't look anywhere else than into his eyes.

'Avanti....' he called. My name became more sweeter, when he called.

'Huh....'

'I love you' he said. I couldn't believe myself on what I heard. I was still looking at his eyes still. He came closer to my face. I closed my eyes. I could feel his breath. Finally our lips met.

#24

I woke up early in the morning. It was the best sleep I had in weeks. My hand was still in his. It could be the best feeling, when you find your loved one next to you when you open your eyes in the morning. I missed that beautiful face. I played with his hair while he was still in his dreams.

'Good morning!' Sanjay came back from his night watching schedule with Kevin.

'Morning. Isn't he awake yet?' Kevin asked.

'No, he was a bit tired.' I said. Kevin laughed and winked at me.

I blushed and said 'Shut up!' Sanjay didn't mind this conversation; he went and woke Geebi and Priya. Sanjay gave the fruits and berries he got.

'We can't stay for much longer here. There aren't enough fruits around here in these trees.' he said.

'I guess Rohit would have plucked all the fruits he needed during his stay here.' Kevin gave his smile and winked again. But I couldn't understand the inner meaning of it this time. We were all waiting for Rohit to tell the missing part of the story. The reason why he had run away, without telling us. We did not want to pry it out from him.

'When he is comfortable, he will tell.' I said when Priya asked me about it.

'What is the confusion here?' Rohit woke up from his sleep.

'Nothing....' Sanjay said. We explained to him about what we were discussing.

'It's ok. You can take your time. We are in no hurry.' I said.

'No Avanti. I am hesitant to tell you all because, you may take it in the wrong sense. But since you have asked, I will tell you.' he said.

'Remember on first day, I came back getting hurt.' He began. We all became quiet to know his story. 'On that day, when I thought of just going around the place, I saw Mohan talking over his walkie talkie. I heard him say, that the Uranium content was very high in these twenty tons and we can get a higher price from the western countries. The man on the other side had asked him to go to the mine site and get it ready by evening.'

'Hang on that's when Anand said that there was an elephant spotted and had asked Mohan to go and check it out.' Geebi brought back our memories. It all made sense now.

He continued, 'I was shocked and followed him. But that's when I tripped and fell. Mohan saw me and brought me back. I couldn't find the place.' he paused.

'When we were going to the Honey falls, I met Gopal from the other group. We were talking about all things, when he opened his map to check how far the falls was from there. That was when I saw the X mark on the map. Since he was under Mohan, I guessed it could be the place where the mine was. So I deliberately exchanged the map with ours'.' He took a break.

'So it wasn't you who drew that X mark on the map?' Sanjay asked.

Rohit shook his head.

'Then on that day in the Honey falls, when Anand came and suggested me to stay back. I don't know why he insisted that I stay back even when I said I was extremely fine. Since Mohan also stayed back during that day, I took this opportunity to know more. After you all left for the falls, Mohan said he had to go back to the check post for some inspection and left. I didn't have to follow him since I had the map. Couple of hours after he left, I said I will get some fruits and left for Adisuri valley.'

He continued. 'It was a different place. You have seen it right?'

We all nodded.

'I observed for a long time, Mohan was not at all to be seen. I thought I had come to a wrong place. Nevertheless, I went down to check the place. When I entered one of their warehouses, I saw some peculiar yellow colour stones.' He said.

'Wait is it this stone you are talking about?' I asked and showed him the stone that Sanjay and I had pocketed from the valley.

He looked at the stone and was shocked. 'How long have you been had it?' he asked.

'A couple of days. Why?' I asked. He took the stone from me and threw it out of the cave.

'What the…. Why did you throw it away? It could be worth something.' Malvika said and got up to search the stone.

Rohit pulled her back. 'Don't bring it, its radioactive.' He said.

'Are you serious? Is it radioactive?' Priya asked.

He nodded. 'It's Uranium ore.'

'The yellow cake' Priya said bringing her subjects expertize into the scene.

Geebi was not satisfied with the conversation. 'What is this yellow cake? Can somebody please explain?'

'Geebi, yellow cake is the ore of uranium. Its Uranium oxide, U_3O_8. It is from this ore we get the nuclear fissile material that could be used for power production.' Priya explained.

'Or to make nuclear weapons.' Rohit said.

'What do Anand and Mohan do with this yellow cake or whatever this ore is called?' Kevin asked.

'I will tell you.' Rohit said and continued with his story. 'When I went near the stone, I heard a ringing noise near the table at the entrance of the warehouse. It was a walkie talkie. I didn't want to turn it on and get into trouble. But human instincts, I pressed the 'receive' button. Mohan on the other end said that he was coming to the warehouse. I realized that there wasn't much time, so I took some pictures of this, took the walkie talkie and went out of the warehouse. But it was too late, Mohan saw me. He chased after me, but instead of following me that idiot went inside the warehouse to check. I got the time and ran away.' He drank some water from the bottle he had.

'What happened to the walkie talkie? You still have it?' I asked.

He nodded and took it out of his bag. The small machine captured my attention immediately. 'Oh this is the Motorola T – 5500 walkie-talkie. No wonder they use it for a long range communication.' Everyone was looking at me as if I was the second Priya.

'I had a friend in the Ham Club who taught me to use this.' I said.

Rohit continued with his story. 'After that I was extremely cautious in my movement. I thought of returning back to the camp, but that's when the walkie talkie beeped again. I once again pressed the 'receive' button. It was Anand's voice, 'Fool why did you let him go. He hasn't returned here yet. Come back to the falls soon. Doubts may arise.' I guess they didn't realize that I had taken away their walkie talkie. So I decided to stay back in the forest for that night. That was when I found out about this place. Next day, I thought that you would have far gone from this forest. But I was shocked when I saw Sanjay near the reservoir. I thought of approaching him. But, Mohan was waiting for me in the reservoir and that's why I couldn't help him when he fainted. Suddenly the walkie talkie beeped again. Mohan was asking whether he could kill Sanjay and put the blame on me. But Anand replied, 'Idiot you have caused enough trouble, don't add more.' So Mohan picked up Sanjay and went back to the base camp. I waited for few more days for help. But none came.' he finished.

'How did you know that we came back?' I asked.

'I was constantly observing the mine area. Village people usually come in the late evening and work the whole night. They pack all the ore in a large container and label it as fish products. One night when I was observing, I saw someone flashing light from top of the hill. I thought of going and seeing it the next day morning. No one was there, but there were evidence that few people had stayed the previous night. A small fire was put up in the top.'

'Oh my God! It was me Rohit. I came that night in the late hours to see the valley. If only I had known you were around.' I said. He smiled and pushed back my hair that was covering my face. 'We even found your shoes.' I exclaimed.

'I hoped that you would remember the shoes.' He winked at me. How could I forget it. He continued with his story, 'Next day Anand was very furious. He called Mohan to come immediately to the mine site. I was hiding in the hill and watching them. Mohan brought the reporter and her cameraman to the centre of the open region and shot them dead.' He said.

'Ya we saw them too.' Kevin said.

'That day evening I heard Anand saying something about bait to capture Rohit. I immediately understood that it must be you guys. So I was waiting for something to happen the whole evening. In the night, Anand brought you and kept you in one of the warehouses. People started coming in the evening to work, so I couldn't do anything. I waited for few days, but he never brought you outside the warehouse.' He took a break. 'One day an old man accidently entered the warehouse, where you were kept. That evening he was killed by Mohan.'

'What! Vasu's dad is dead?' Priya was shaken on hearing the news.

Rohit went ahead with his story. 'That night Mohan had brought the bodies of the reporter and the cameraman near the hill and buried them. I went later and took out his camera's memory card. As Anand used to call him, he is really a fool. Next day morning when they dug up the body, he found the memory card was missing. He knew I was around. Mohan went inside the warehouse, to check whether I was there or not, I suppose.' We nodded, acknowledging him. He continued. 'That was when he brought you out. I got an idea and went near the main fuse of the power source.'

'Yes, I was wondering how they get the power inside the forest.' Priya asked.

'How else…. Hydroelectric power plant in Honey falls.' Rohit said. 'So as I was saying, I went and waited near the main fuse for some time. And at the proper moment, I pulled the fuse, shutting down the entire plant. And rest as you know is history.' He finished.

'And how come the water of the reservoir is so dirty and full of froth?' Sanjay asked.

'That is because, to clean the ore, they need lots of clean water. Where do they have to go, when they have this big reservoir inside the forest without anyone's notice.' Rohit replied.

I went near him. It was a happy feeling, just to be with him. 'So you have the memory card?' Sanjay asked. Rohit nodded.

'Good then we have to somehow escape from this place and give the memory card to the police. They will do the necessary.' Malvika became enthusiastic.

'Then what are we waiting for, let's go' Geebi said.

#25

Geebi and Kevin went to get the necessary things for our visit back to the village. It was Rohit's idea to go back to the village, when he got this piece of information from the walkie talkie. It was Anand's voice again from it.

'Mohan, we have another problem now. Since that Rohit and friends haven't returned, their parents have organized a press meet. As a result, there will be another special task force team coming to help us find them. They will be in the village today evening. I will try to convince them that the forest is very dangerous and we can handle it on our own.' There was a break in the voice, 'Just in case, shut down all the equipment and immediately transport all the containers to Cochin.' It ended.

'If we get a chance to talk to the special task team, before Anand or Mohan talk to them, we can convince them.' Rohit said. But the problem was reaching on time.

If we take the longer way by going on the other side of the hill, it will be safer but we may not reach on time to meet the special team. But on the other hand, if we go through this side the hill, we may risk ourselves by getting caught by them in the same mine site.

'Let us vote on it!' Sanjay said. 'Those in favour of taking the shorter, but dangerous route' he said and raised his hand. Kevin' hand went up immediately, followed by mine and Rohit's. The other three preferred the longer route, despite taking a larger time to reach.

In the end it was decided. We were risking ourselves to reach the village on time. The clouds were gathering unusually in the noon time. We left the cave and carefully climbed down the hill.

We were walking along the river to reach the Adisuri valley. The water in the river was pure. It was not mixed with the dirt from cleaning the ore.

'Rohit did you ever think that we would come back for you?' Malvika asked.

'If anyone of you were like this, I would have not gone home without you people.' He smiled. Kevin came and hugged him. Sanjay joined them and Geebi too. This was the first time I was seeing guys hugging like this. I never knew guys were this emotional.

'Guys, careful. We are nearing the mine site.' Priya warned. As expected there was no one at the mine site. Anand would not have wanted his man to be in the mine site, when the special task team was inspecting. The lights weren't on today. The image of Mohan pulling the trigger over those two reporters was not leaving my head. I gripped Rohit's hand tightly. He smiled. It was really amazing to be like this. I wished the time would freeze at that moment; free from the annoying mobile phone, hectic city life, troubles and even responsibilities.

Sanjay was holding the walkie talkie and checking something on it. 'Does Anand know that you have this walkie talkie?' he asked.

'I don't think so. If he had known, he wouldn't have discussed such matters with Mohan through this.' Rohit said.

Sanjay was not satisfied. 'Anyway we should to be careful.'

'Chill bro! I don't think he is that clever.' Kevin said. Maybe he was right. We crossed the mine site without any trouble. Once again the stinking smell penetrated our nostrils, indicating that the reservoir was not far away.

'Gosh! The reeking smell' Malvika closed her face with the dupatta.

'Guys I never asked you, how did you come back here?' Rohit asked.

'Oh! That's a long story bro.' Kevin said and looked at me. Rohit noticed Kevin looking at me.

'I am in all ears to listen. Besides we have a long way to go.' Rohit said and noticed my face shrink. He asked me what had happened. I didn't say anything.

'Why don't you say Avanti!' Kevin said. I smiled at him. I don't think his anger had vanished yet. Rohit suddenly put his hand over my shoulder. He was playing with my hair and gently pulled my long strands down. I was literally mesmerized by his action.

'Ya why don't you tell me Avanti.' He asked putting across his handsome face across me. I explained to him, from what had happened from the day he left to the time we got caught by Anand.

'You jumped from the running train?' Rohit panicked. 'How is your hand now?'

'It was nothing. The doctors exaggerated it.' I smiled. He took my hand to inspect and closely massaged my hand.

'Ahem…. Ahem….Enough of your romance' Kevin winked at him. He blushed.

The sky was getting dark. We don't have any navigational aids to help us. When the sun was up, we knew. But when the sun set, there was really nothing except the stars.

'Guys hold your hands and walk! It is pitch dark.' Sanjay said. We couldn't risk using the torch lights. Also there wasn't enough power left in it to operate for long.

'Stop! Are we heading in the correct direction?' Priya asked.

'I hope so.' Sanjay said.

'Rohit do you remember which way is the village?' Geebi asked.

'I think we were heading east.' Rohit replied.

'Then follow me.' Said Geebi. 'We can look at the stars and find the direction.' Geebi's interest in astronomy had us helped when in need.

'Is it right Geebi?' Malvika was not happy with trusting the stars.

'You don't have to trust me, but rely on them.' he pointed over the carpet of stars in the clear sky. We went ahead in the way Geebi had pointed.

'Hey look at the lights. That must be the village.' Priya beamed. Finally we were all happy. There was a possibility for us to go back home. At that moment, the walkie talkie creaked with its ringing tone. Rohit looked at us and pressed the 'receive' button.

'Rohit we are not as foolish as you thought.' It echoed with Anand's voice. He looked at us. All of us expressed the same shock. But the voice continued, 'Did you think that we would let you go away that easily?'

'Let's run to the village' Rohit whispered.

'That won't be so easy.' Anand from walkie-talkie spoke. His voice was making my spine cold. We have easily been fallen into their trap. Sanjay was right. We should have listened to him. He was in the same shock as everyone was.

'Sorry bro!' Kevin apologized to Sanjay.

'This is not the time you idiot!' he was searching for Anand and Mohan.

'Rohit tell your friend not to search anymore!' his voice spoke again from the walkie talkie. Then he appeared from our side and Mohan from the other.

'Too many mistakes and too much problems have been caused!' Anand looked at Mohan. He continued, 'Nevertheless, we will brand you as murderers before the task force comes here.' He paused, 'Yes they are not coming today.'

There were several lights moving towards us from the hill side. It was like a line of fire that was travelling among the forest. Anand didn't seem to notice it.

'In all my four years in the mine, no one has made it alive after knowing the truth.' He said. 'Mohan, if you please.' Mohan raised his gun and pointed on us. The lights were getting closer. It was not until it was few hundred feet distance, the lights turned out to be fire sticks that the village men carry in their hand. They were walking towards us. Mohan dropped the gun down.

'Let us get out of here.' I said. Before Anand or Mohan could react, the village people reached them. We ran and away from them, but don't know which way to go. There was no time for Geebi to calculate the direction from stars.

'Ayya! Vasu voda appa kaanom. Adhan oor makkal ellam serinthu poi thaedalamnu' a village man was saying that Vasu's father is missing, so the village people were planning to search for him on their own.

We were hiding and listening to what was happening out there. Anand immediately turned the table across us. He said, 'that is what I was enquiring these college students. Wait…. Where are they?' he asked Mohan.

'Sir, they ran away….' Mohan hung his face down.

'What the…. Are you crazy? You know what they have done right?'

'What have they done sir?' asked one of the village man in Tamil.

'They have killed that fellow; Vasu's father. Mohan has seen it.' He lied coldly. 'They are terrorists; camouflaged with the college students and entered our forest.'

There was no more reason for us to stay back. And the entire village might come against us. We went back into the forest. Our only hope of going back had been shattered. Also we had been branded as terrorists.

#26

'There is no way we are going to go out of this forest, without getting caught.' Malvika was heartbroken. We were running back to the cave. Again the walkie talkie rang.

'Throw that stupid machine away.' I screamed. Priya plucked it from Rohit's hand and pressed the 'receive' button.

'You are a coward. Are you listening, you are a coward Anand. Killing innocent people and living a life out of it. And causing a hundred more to suffer with unbearable pain and making them homeless. Is this how you treat the village that raised you? What mistake did Veera's mother do? What did Vasu's father do? And who gave you the right to take the life of those people. You are inhuman. You don't deserve to be the forest guard.' Priya thundered over the walkie talkie. She stabbed it back into Rohit's hand and walked away. 'I have had enough.' She murmured. There was only silence from the other end. Was he even listening to what Priya had been saying?

'Don't speak as if you know everything.' The voice from the other side was broken. 'You haven't lived our lives. So think before....' Rohit threw it hard on the ground before Anand could complete. We haven't been ever more silent like this before. We didn't mind taking the longer route to reach the cave. And the remaining life in our torch batteries drained off.

'Wait!' I said and ran back.

'Avanti! What happened?' Rohit chased me behind. I was searching for it.

'Avanti stop.' Rohit had reached me. 'Are you insane? Why are you running?'

'The walkie talkie! We have to find it.' I said.

'What the.... Why do we have to?' Rohit was asking. I found it in two pieces, hanging together by one or two wires. I pressed all those wiring inside and pressed the 'on' button. It glowed. 'Perfect! Let's go' I said. Rohit didn't bother me. I guess he thought I turned nuts.

'What happened?' Priya was worried. I didn't reply.

'Apparently she went back to get the walkie talkie.' Rohit said.

'Why do you need this thing?' Priya stormed in. I immediately removed the batteries from it and switched it to our torch. And it obviously glowed. Priya stepped back and even Rohit put up a smile. I gave it to Sanjay as he was in the front. When I was about the throw the walkie talkie away, it seized my attention. The small module, that was in the lower right side of the walkie talkie.

'Guys I guess we are being watched.' I blurted out. 'This is a next gen GPS locator. This is not a part of this walkie talkie.' Suddenly I felt a pair of eyes looking at us from the dark background. Our evil mind creates the scene, that we fear the most.

'So that means he would know about the cave.' Sanjay asked. Probably he would have known. What if he is waiting for us there? 'Why to risk by going back? Let us camp somewhere else for the night.'

We walked till the Sittraru River and camped on the banks there. It was very open. But we didn't have any other place to go and our hunger was taking its toll.

'We have to survive with this water for the night.' Geebi said. At least the water here was pure and drinkable. Priya and Geebi were staying guard for the night. In no more than minutes I fell asleep.

I was scared. Tears were trickling down my eyes. I held his hand and ran as fast as I could, without looking back. But there was something I had left behind, which was very important to me. My eyes automatically opened without knowing what it was. Once again I failed to know what it was.

I couldn't sleep. Sleep and appetite were never staying with me. I went and sat with Priya on the river bank. She was watching her reflection from the water under moon light.

'No one can communicate with us right? Will we be hiding our whole life like this?' Priya asked.

'No Priya we will find a way. You will surely get back to your family.' I replied. But deep inside my mind, I feared the same thing. What if we are stuck in this forest for our whole life time?

'But I like this life. This village, forest and this unusual silence. It just makes me feel that the life in our city is far worse than I thought it was.' Priya said. It was true. More than running for my life, I understood a lot. I can't imagine getting a clear glass of water in city, in the open. To make a drinking water drinkable, it has to undergo so many processes. In the end what we are getting is not just water, but a solution of all those chemicals that makes it look clean.

'Hey what were you saying?' I beamed.

'What was I…. Oh about the calm environment here and….' Priya was saying. But I don't want that.

'Not that Priya….You said that no one communicate with us right.' I was in my own thought process.

'Yes. Isn't it true?' She was confused.

'Yes…. No one has to communicate with us. But we can communicate with others.' I said.

'What…. Are you sleep-talking Avanti? How is it possible?' She asked.

'I will explain. Wake the others up.' I knew what to do next.

#27

'What is it Avanti? Can't it wait till the morning? I haven't slept in ages.' Malvika was not ready to get up. But she got used to sleeping on hard grounds. From her cosy silk mattress in her house to this stone bed was a drastic change for her. But Kevin was not confined with all these. He took a handful of cold river water and splashed it on her face. Her adrenaline would have pumped hard to realize what has happened.

'What the…. Kevin!' she shouted. But he calmly went near her and kissed on her cheeks. She blushed. She wrapped her hand around him. They both forgot that we were around them.

'Ahem…. Guys I don't think this is the time!' Sanjay was giving that sarcastic look in his face. I looked at Rohit. He elegantly winked at me.

'It's now or never mate.' Kevin slightly punched on Sanjay's chest.

'Guys lets come back to business.' Geebi said. 'Avanti let's hear what you have to say.'

'I was thinking that….' I was hesitant to say it. Everyone's eyes were glued on me. 'I have a plan for us to escape from this place. But….'

'But…. But what?' Priya asked.

'Until I feel it's the right time to say, no one should ask me about it.' I said. It's for their own safety that I am making them deficit of information.

'You have really turned nuts Avanti. What is this big secret that you are hiding from us?' Kevin was not happy with this.

'You have to trust me in this Kevin.' I replied. He was silent.

'I trust her.' Rohit said and came and stood by my side. He gave all the assurance I needed. 'I do too.' Sanjay said and came by my side. Priya and Geebi joined too. Kevin just breathed, 'Ok fine' and went near the river. I was worried that I am hurting him again.

'He will turn around.' Priya said. 'So what's the plan Captain?' Priya nudged me with the elbow. 'First we have to collect some wood to burn.' I said.

'For what?' Sanjay asked. I gave him a stern look. 'It's ok, I don't have to know now.' He backed off. Rohit and Priya were laughing seeing it.

Next day morning Sanjay and Rohit left early to collect some logs of wood. Kevin didn't say much. He was busy gathering some food for us to eat. I was wondering when Kevin would become the Kevin he was before this trip. Everything was normal before the trip. Instead of creating a leisure time for us, the trip had only caused a lot of problems for us.

'Hey Avanti what's that worrying your mind that you keep a secret from us?' Priya asked. I don't know how she senses it, but she finds out exactly when something is bothering me.

'Nothing dear.' I said and smiled.

'If you don't want to tell me, that's fine.' She said and walked away.

Its words like these from your best friend that affect you more than anything. 'Wait.' I said. She stopped and looked at me. 'It's not that I don't want to tell you Priya, but I am scared myself if it will work or not. That is why I am hesitant to share it with all you people.' I said.

'Unless you tell us what the plan is, there won't be any unity among us.' She said.

'I will compose myself and say it soon.' I tried to escape.

'Ok fine.' She said. I could sense that she was not happy. But more than her happiness, it was the success of my plan that was important. After that nobody questioned me about anything. Rohit and Sanjay fully trusted my decisions.

It was late afternoon, when everyone had brought whatever I had asked them to get.

'Guys we are going to set fire to a part of this forest tomorrow.' I said.

'And you won't explain why we have to do this.' Kevin pointed his voice from back. I nodded negatively. 'I don't know where this is going to end.' he blabbered and went to bring some woods.

'Forget about him. So which part of the forest are you planning to burn?' Sanjay asked.

'The Vettumalai cave.' I replied.

#28

'That will be last thing we should do.' Geebi said. 'If Anand knows about the GPS device, he will track us down to the cave.'

'Yes that is exactly what I want him to do.' I said calmly.

'And if Anand catches us there, how are you planning to escape?' he asked.

'We won't get caught. Trust me.' I said. 'We have to split ourselves into three groups. Geebi and Priya, you both will have to go to the cave and burn the firewood. Burn it only till the smoke rises and leave the place immediately. Malvika and Kevin, both of you will stay in the village temple with the walkie-talkie.' I paused for a moment. 'Rohit and Sanjay will join me in executing my plan.' I finished.

'That's interesting!' said Sanjay. I smiled at him.

'But before that we have to go to village and stay over there for the night.' I said.

'Why is that I find all your suggestions lead us nowhere but getting us caught easily.' Kevin was still not happy about the way the plan was going. I could not blame him either. If I was in his shoes, I would have acted similarly.

'No Kevin! It would be better for us in the end.' I said, trying to convince him. But he had fixed in his mind that whatever decisions I made would be wrong.

'Say it to yourself! I am not going to that village again. You heard him right. The whole village will be against us for what they think we did to Vasu's father.' He said. But before I could argue with him more, Malvika interrupted him. She told something in his ears. He seems to listen to it intensively.

In the end of it, Kevin gave a positive smile. 'We will take care of it!' Malvika gave me thumbs up. I let out a sigh of relief.

'But where are we going to stay in the village, without getting caught from them?' Rohit asked.

'In the temple, of course. It will be closed during these months. Remember?' I asked. Everybody nodded.

We trekked back to the village and made sure that no one saw us while we were climbing. The temple was, as expected, locked. Its high compound walls were difficult to climb up. We managed with the help of some logs of wood. Nothing had changed in the temple interiors. We slept for the night inside one of the Mandaps.

*   *   *   *

We could see the smoke rising from far north. Geebi and Priya would have done a very good work.

'I hope they return on time….' I was telling Rohit.

'Don't worry! They will be alright. Now tell me what we have to do?' he asked.

'I will tell you on the way.' I said and turned to face Kevin. But he didn't bother to look at me. I turned to Malvika, 'Before that, Malvika stay inside the temple all the time. Until we come back, don't come out of it.' I said and went ahead with Rohit and Sanjay.

'Bro! If we pull this through, we will party!' said Rohit.

'Sure thing bro.' Kevin winked at him. We climbed the wall and came out of the temple.

'Will you tell us at least now? Where are we going?' Sanjay asked.

'Will tell you! In the meantime, remove your overcoat and leave it here.' I said.

He was removing it as I said, but still asked 'Why?'

'It will lead them on the trail towards the temple.' I said. He was confused, but threw the overcoat near an old banyan tree near the temple. I decided that there is no point in delaying them more without information.

'We are going to the village now.' I said.

'Have you really gone crazy, Avanti?' Rohit went to pick up the overcoat that Sanjay had dropped on the ground.

'No don't pick it up. Let it lie there.' I said. But he had picked it up and dusted the dirt off it. 'What if I tell you that both Mohan and Anand won't be there in the village!'

'How is that possible....Oh wait, the smoke, they would have gone to the caves!' Rohit finally reasoned it out.

'Brilliant!' I said.

'But it still doesn't explain why we are going to the village.' He asked.

'To send the information through Ham radio!' I said.

#29

'You are really....the best Avanti. Completely brilliant.' Sanjay said. I blushed.

'Hang on! Why are they both staying in the temple?' Rohit asked. 'That too with the walkie talkie.'

'I need a diversion. That's why.' I said.

'What if they get caught?' Sanjay asked.

'They won't. Remember the temple is closed. If they have to open it, they have to call the whole village. Before that we will be done with our work here.' I replied.

We were hiding behind the brick building which was closer to Mohan's house. All the people were in the centre of the village to celebrate their festival. Still it wasn't easy to go inside the village. Few suspicious eyes were watching us. But we managed not to stay long inside the village. The sky was getting darker and darker. We were watching if there was any activity around Mohan's house from the brick building.

'Let's go.' I said. When we were sure that no one was there, we went ahead to his house. It wasn't locked. We were not surprised, as the villagers always kept their house unlocked as there was no fear of theft. We went inside the house. It was like the way I had remembered it. 'They won't. Remember the temple is closed. If they have to open it, they have to call the whole village. Before that we will be done with our work here.' I replied. 'Also if they both roam around anywhere in the village or forest, there is a possibility that they may get caught.' I said. 'It's safe for them there than anywhere else.'

'Where is this radio Avanti?' Sanjay asked.

'It's in the second room. Over here.' We went inside the room. There was no electricity in the village. We had to light a log of wood to keep to see around. Rohit dipped one end of the wood in the wax that was kept at one end of the room and lighted it. Mohan had beautifully arranged this room. In the centre of the room was this huge machine that had always captured my attention. In the back drop, he had arranged many tusks and skulls of various animals. There wasn't any window in this room. But he had ventilated this room with small rectangular holes in the top. In the left wall, he had arranged many books and on the right there were maps and guns hanging. In front of the machine there was a small chair made of wood and a table which had a microphone and a headset on it. I was mesmerized with the beauty of this room.

'Avanti do your stuff. There isn't enough time.' Sanjay said. I realized that I always wanted a room like this and have this kind of huge Ham radio with me. I went in searching for the power button. I wasn't familiar with using these complicated gizmos. My radio was small but easy to operate.

'Sanjay can you search those shelves for any instruction manual?' I asked.

'What? You don't know to operate this? Mohan himself had explained it to you right!' Sanjay asked.

'I wasn't listening, remember! Veera's mom died that day.' I said. I know the protocol to be followed, but I have to change the frequency from Mohan to mine so that I can broadcast. He went on searching for it. Rohit joined him in the search.

'Found it!' Rohit beamed.

'Excellent, now find how to change the pre-set frequency.' I said and turned on the machine and wore the headphone. There was full static from the headphones. I reduced the volume and wore the headphones.

'How does he get electricity for this to run?' Sanjay asked.

'It is from the solar panels and the batteries. It requires very less power.' I replied, pointing to the cable coming out of the machine. Rohit was still searching from the manual. I got up and plucked the book from him. I searched the manual; it explained about different models that the company had to offer and the benefits of one over the other. 'Instructions! Turn to the instructions page.' I said to myself. 'There it is!' I beamed. Sanjay and Rohit came around me. But it had three different model's instruction.

'Class of the machine!' I said and searched on the machine, if anything was instructed on it. It was near the microphone the letters CX2 was etched.

'It's CX2 variant.' I once again searched on the manual. I pressed the buttons like it was given in the manual. Then the small LED screen glowed with 'enter the new frequency'.

I entered 56.8 and pressed the start button. No one was listening from other end.

'Hello! Hello! Mercury here!' I said. There was no reply. I turned to Rohit and said 'No one is listening.' His face was down. My normal session will be from six in the evening. The wall clock is showing only 5 45. But I didn't stop.

'Hello! Hello! Anyone there? Mercury here. This is an SOS call! Anyone there?' Still the listeners' number was showing zero.

'Hello is anyone out there? Please help! We are in danger.' Once again I made a mistake. I am going to be the cause of my friends' death.

'Hello! This is Mercury here….. Is anyone….'

Suddenly the static got reduced and there were fine grains of voices. 'Go ahead…. Mercury! ….is the SOS call….' The listeners' number increased to one.

'Oh my God, someone is online.' I almost cried.

'Hello this is Mercury here! We are in grave danger. Someone please help us.'

'Mercury…. What….help you want? What danger….' The listener's voice cracked in the headphones.

'We are in Thirunelveli district forest, the Meakery village.' I said.

'co….dinates.'

'Sorry say again….'

'Your coordinates….Mercury where you are exactly and what is your trouble….' The voice became clear. It was a shaken lady voice. I guess it must be the old couple from Bengaluru.

'Coordinates?' I was surprised. I didn't know the coordinates of this place.

'Wait…. You need coordinates of what?' Rohit asked.

'My listener needs coordinates for this place.' I looked at him disappointedly. But he went near the wall and pointed his finger on the map and searched the Lat and Long of this place. I conveyed whatever he said to me.

'….this is my coordinates, and we are attacked by Forest rangers and guards. They are selling our resources to foreign countries.'

'I will see what…. ' there was a thud on the door. Anand, not Mohan was standing at the door.

'Didn't expect me here right? All your plans are getting foiled, I know.' he said. He was in the first room and Rohit put out the flame. How could he have known? I made sure that no one knows this. Even if anyone of us get caught, it would be only me they would want and not my friends. 'I know that you have hidden some of your friends in the temple too. But in vain! Mohan has gone to take care of them. Now come out. Don't waste my time.' He came inside the second room. It was pitch dark except for the light from the machine. He looked around and saw me.

'What the hell are you doing!' he thrashed me to the ground. My head hit the ground very hard. I was struggling to get up. He was trying to turn off the machine.

'You idiots! What have you been doing on this?' he said and pulled out his gun. 'Were you talking to someone?' My listener was still listening to these. He lifted me up and hit me in the head with the trigger.

'Rohit where are you? I have got your friend here. Come out and I am not going to wait long again.' He said. He was holding me by my neck. I couldn't see Rohit and Sanjay. It was pitch dark everywhere. 'If you are wondering how I found you, check your shoe sole. The GPS was not only in the walkie talkie, but also in your shoes.' He said.

I guess he would have put it when he found the shoes before us. My entire plan was to divert them so that we could have escaped from this place. But it's all in vain now. All of a sudden there was a huge fire that encapsulated the corner of the room. But still both of them were not to be seen. The fire was getting bigger and bigger. Someone had burnt the entire wax vessel.

'Rohit!' Anand screamed.

Then there was a hard push on Anand. His hand holding my neck loosened and he fell to the ground. Rohit held my hand and barged out of the second room. The main entrance door was locked. Sanjay came out of the second room crawling. And fell down against the wall.

'Sanjay are you alright?' I asked. There was no response.

'Haha haha! Fools you can't escape.' came Anand's voice from inside. He came outside pointing the gun at us. But this time he didn't hesitate. He pulled the trigger straight at me.

But nothing happened. Except Rohit was bleeding on the ground. My world had come to stand still. I couldn't believe my eyes. There was severe puncture in this chest. His blood was flowing like a river under him.

'Avanti….Avanti I love you.' He said.

'Don't worry Rohit….It.. it will be fine. Rohit….' I had to stop the blood. I didn't know how I was going to do it.

'Avanti…. Listen….Avanti the wax will explode…. explode now. I can't come. The bullet…. gone deep.' He said. 'Go…. Leave….'

Then the silence struck me.

Sanjay

#30

I could hear Avanti crying amidst the fierce crackling of the flames. What had happened? And the pungent smoke was starting to choke me. Both my knees were hurting.

'Sanjay….Sanjay….' Avanti was stroking my shoulders. I opened my eyes. She was crying uncontrollably. 'Sanjay…. Come let's go!' she said and took my hand and dragged me out of the building. I got up and leaned on her shoulders. She pulled me to the door and out of it. Near the door, there was lot of blood. I looked at Avanti, checking if she had any wounds. Behind her, Rohit was lying down in the pool of blood. But she wasn't even looking at his side.

'Rohit….Rohit….' I called. There was no response from him.

'Avanti…. Rohit?' I asked. She was crying even more loudly and pushed me outside the house. She made me sit outside the house against a tree.

'Avanti…. Rohit. He is hurt badly.' I said and got up to go inside.

'Rohit is dead Sanjay…. He is go…ne.' She fell on her knees and started crying. 'My Rohit is no more. He is no more Sanjay….' she was banging her head on the floor. 'It's all because of me. If I hadn't brought him here, he would have been happily living. If I hadn't brought him here, he wouldn't have taken a bullet for me.'

'Avanti…. Stop…. Avanti please Avanti….' I was struggling to raise her up. The world was falling apart. My best friend has died. Avantika was unable to control herself. I was feeling an inner rage. How can he destroy my friend's life? How much hopes would he have had. All his dreams are shattered now. His wonderful life that was ahead of him, is now gone. I got up to go inside his house. Then suddenly there was this bang! The house exploded. Debris was falling over us. I went and covered Avanti. She kept crying like anything. I just couldn't imagine how her life will be hereafter.

I lifted her up and made her walk. 'Avanti….Please get up Avanti!' She was not ready to move away from the place.

'Sanjay bring Rohit back….I want him back…. I want my Rohit back. I have to plead him sorry.' She trembled inconsolably. I really couldn't do anything. Tears were dripping down my face. It was going to be a life without my best friend.

'Avanti…. Let's go back Avanti.' I said. 'Else there won't be any use in the sacrifice Rohit made.'

'It's my fault entirely. If I hadn't called him to come….' She was yet to come out of the trauma.

'Let us get back Avanti before the villagers come to this place.' I was pleading. I slowly made her walk along the unlit path to the temple.

*   *   *   *

The plan had worked, but at the cost of Rohit's life. The old people from Bengaluru who were listening to Avanti's broadcast had the recorded evidence of the scene in Mohan's house. The special task force came and seized the mine and took Mohan under custody. Anand was burnt to death from the fire. The village people were happy that they would get proper water to drink hereafter. The whole of national media were gathered to know about the students who were framed as terrorists. Our parents came too. It was very hard to see Rohit's parents and to explain to them what had happened.

'Have you seen Avanti?' Priya asked. 'She has been missing from morning.' Malvika came to the brick building, where all the reporters, our parents and the collector had halted.

'She left us!' Malvika gave the letter. 'Found it in her bag.' I plucked the letter from her. It was her handwriting, I could easily tell. It read,

My dear friends,

Sometimes what we wish for is too high to reach. But we never stop until we reach it. What I wished for is of similar kind. Even when it was at a reachable distance, I didn't get it. If there is anyone to blame for his death, it would be me. I know you all will be saying otherwise, especially you, Sanjay. But I need some escape from this normal life. I am not going to make a stupid decision like suicide. All I need is to break-away from all the troubles I caused. So don't try to contact me.

Love you loads
Avanti

I read it and reread it again and again. But she wasn't going to come back. She had chosen her way of life.

People have walked in all sorts of paths. Some choose easy ones, some prefer the rough one and some even walk the un-walkable. But all we did was walk a little gentler on this forest.

Epilogue….

Four months later….

'Is it true?' Priya was asking me.

'Yes I am damn sure. It's her voice only.' I said.

'So when is the time she normally broadcasts?' Malvika asked. We were seated in the cafeteria. Being in final year of engineering means you have more free hours and even more project work. Geebi was getting his favourite onion pakodas.

'Should start any minute now!' I said. We were sitting in front of my laptop. Technology had developed; now we could listen to people broadcasting through Ham via our laptops. We just had to set the frequency. It was difficult task finding the correct frequency in which she broadcasted. Only guess was that she still broadcasts at the same time – Fridays at six.

'Did she say anything on where she is now?' Kevin asked.

'Nope….' I replied.

Then it started. Her sweet mesmerizing voice was reverberating from the speakers.

'Good evening my dear listeners. It's your Mercury again with a new topic…Today I am going to take you back in history to the time of Ramayana. Remember Lord Rama went to Lanka to kill the mighty king Ravana. Well that was not the only story that happened during that time. At the same time, there was a small coastal city in the southern India ruled by a King. It was known for its rich mineral resources. One of its resources was Thorium, a black silvery material that could be used for nuclear warfare.

We all have known about Brahmastra as a nuclear weapon. Our Gods have used it to destroy evil and bring peace in the country. And our ancient textbooks and puranas have depicted that these powerful weapons were obtained from Lord Brahma on praying to him. But isn't it too much to ask from a God to obtain such a powerful weapon?

When Rama prayed to Lord Varuna, the king of oceans and rain, he didn't answer his prayers. He took one of his powerful bow and arrow and sent it like thunderbolts of Indra into the sea. The Ocean was badly shaken up and all the animals and fish were disturbed and perturbed. The water had receded much into the ocean. Still there wasn't any response from Lord Varuna. So Rama took out the Brahmastra and stretched his bow, aiming at the sea. The whole celestial creations were shaking. Scared Lord Varuna came out of the sea and blessed Rama to build a bridge to Lanka. Rama did not want to waste the Brahmastra. Varuna had asked Rama to send it to Dhrumatulya which was filled with evil people and Rama did so. That place became a desert. But what was the result of the first arrow that Rama used? It created huge waves called Tsunamis that destroyed the small kingdom that was manufacturing these weapons.

And the hard facts are presently discovered by our archaeologists. The receded water has created the huge wave that took over a coastal city. Also the place where Rama has sent the Brahmastra is present day Thar Desert, Rajasthan.

But the King of the coastal city was clever. He had removed most of the thorium from the coastal soil and deposited them deep inside the Western Ghats. During all these years the mineral had absorbed neutrons, a sub atomic particle and transformed into fissile Uranium. An average physics student knows the power of such fissile material.

After the incident in the Mundanthurai forest in 2013, the Government has taken over the mine. But no one bothers about the missing piece of history that has been revealed from this incident. The Meakery village people are the direct descendants from the people who lived in that coastal city.

But what is their condition now? They are still suffering from the skin cancer and impure water.

Who should be blamed for this? Is it the king of the coastal city, who manufactured that deadly weapon? Is it Lord Rama, who aimed the weapon in the seas? Or is it Lord Varuna, who hadn't stopped Rama's action in the first hand? Or is it those two culprits, who were selling those minerals to western countries? Or is it even the Government that has taken over the mine and continues mining minerals from it?

Everyone was following what they thought was right. To them, they were on their path to Dharma. But which is universally right? I leave your mind to dwell over it.

Let us hear what my first listener has to say. Hello!'

'Hello Avantika, I completely agree on what you said about the two culprits.' Came a familiar voice.